He Wanted To Be With Katherine.

Bryce's wild thoughts brought a sudden twist to his lips. He hadn't been this foolhardy in so long he'd forgotten how it felt. He had none other than one wild redhead to thank for that.

A divorced redhead, to boot.

Katherine's past didn't matter. It wasn't as if he were going to fall in love with her and marry her. Heck no, he wasn't.

He just wanted to be with her, to share some of her zest for life. And he wouldn't apologize for doing so. He'd just have to be careful. He'd always been a private person, and the fact that he was a minister didn't mean that he couldn't have a life of his own.

And secrets.

For now, Katherine Mays was going to be *his* best kept secret.

Dear Reader,

Our 20th anniversary pledge to you, our devoted readers, is a promise to continue delivering passionate, powerful, provocative love stories from your favorite Silhouette Desire authors for all the years to come!

As an anniversary treat, we've got a special book for you from the incomparable Annette Broadrick. *Marriage Prey* is a romance between the offspring of two couples from Annette's earliest Desire books, which Silhouette reissued along with a third early Desire novel last month as *Maximum Marriage: Men on a Mission*. Bestselling author Mary Lynn Baxter brings you November's MAN OF THE MONTH...*Her Perfect Man*. A minister and a reformed party girl fall for each other in this classic opposites-attract love story. *A Cowboy's Gift* is the latest offering by RITA Award winner Anne McAllister in her popular CODE OF THE WEST miniseries.

Another RITA winner, Caroline Cross, delivers the next installment of the exciting Desire miniseries FORTUNE'S CHILDREN: THE GROOMS with *Husband—or Enemy?* Dixie Browning's miniseries THE PASSIONATE POWERS continues with *The Virgin and the Vengeful Groom,* part of our extra-sensual BODY & SOUL promotion. And Sheri WhiteFeather has created another appealing Native American hero in *Night Wind's Woman*.

So please join us in celebrating twenty glorious years of category romance by indulging yourself with all six of these compelling love stories from Silhouette Desire!

Enjoy!

Joan Marlow Golan

Joan Marlow Golan
Senior Editor, Silhouette Desire

Please address questions and book requests to:
Silhouette Reader Service
U.S.: 3010 Walden Ave., P.O. Box 1325, Buffalo, NY 14269
Canadian: P.O. Box 609, Fort Erie, Ont. L2A 5X3

Her Perfect Man
MARY LYNN BAXTER

Published by Silhouette Books
America's Publisher of Contemporary Romance

SILHOUETTE BOOKS

ISBN 0-373-76328-X

HER PERFECT MAN

Copyright © 2000 by Mary Lynn Baxter

All rights reserved. Except for use in any review, the reproduction
or utilization of this work in whole or in part in any form by any
electronic, mechanical or other means, now known or hereafter
invented, including xerography, photocopying and recording, or in
any information storage or retrieval system, is forbidden without
the written permission of the editorial office, Silhouette Books,
300 East 42nd Street, New York, NY 10017 U.S.A.

All characters in this book have no existence outside the imagination of
the author and have no relation whatsoever to anyone bearing the same
name or names. They are not even distantly inspired by any individual
known or unknown to the author, and all incidents are pure invention.

This edition published by arrangement with Harlequin Books S.A.

® and TM are trademarks of Harlequin Books S.A., used under license.
Trademarks indicated with ® are registered in the United States Patent
and Trademark Office, the Canadian Trade Marks Office and in other
countries.

Visit Silhouette at www.eHarlequin.com

Printed in U.S.A.

Books by Mary Lynn Baxter

MARY LYNN BAXTER

A native Texan, Mary Lynn Baxter knew instinctively that books would occupy an important part of her life. Always an avid reader, she became a school librarian, then a bookstore owner, before writing her first novel.

Now Mary Lynn Baxter is an award-winning author who has written more than thirty novels, many of which have appeared on the *USA Today* bestseller list.

IT'S OUR 20ᵗʰ ANNIVERSARY!
We'll be celebrating all year,
Continuing with these fabulous titles,
On sale in November 2000.

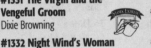

One

The violent flash of lightning, followed by a loud clap of thunder, forced a pause in his thoughts. The Reverend Bryce Burnette swiveled in his office chair and stared outside, where he came face-to-face with another burst of crackling light. He flinched inwardly, feeling as if the sky were closing in on him. At the same time, the sight was beautiful and exhilarating.

East Texas in the fall had a reputation for its storms. Today certainly left that reputation intact.

However, the weather was not his main concern, but rather the young couple in front of him whom he was counseling for their upcoming marriage. With that in mind, he once again gave them his full attention.

"Do you have any questions you'd like to ask?"

Before either of them could respond, another brilliant flash of lightning, followed closely by a ferocious clap of thunder, drew all eyes to the window.

"Mother Nature's sure pitching a fit," Bryce said. "But at least we're getting that much-needed rain." As he turned back to the couple, he noticed that Pam had shrunk against Randy.

"Don't worry, honey," the groom-to-be said, his arm tightening around her shoulders protectively. "You know how these East Texas storms are."

"You think we're safe?" she asked, sounding almost childlike in her nervousness.

Randy gave her another squeeze. "You bet," he answered with all the confidence of a young man who was yet to face any of life's proverbial slings and arrows.

Bryce hid a smile at the expression on Randy's face as his fiancée gazed up at him as though he were God, Jr. Suddenly an old sadness assailed him. Watching them, he couldn't help but remember how good it had felt to have someone cling to and look so trustingly at him.

It had been a long time since that had happened. He'd experienced lonely years of empty arms and silent rooms.

Anxious to escape the unhappy memories, Bryce addressed the couple again. "Now, where were we? I'm sure—"

BOOM!

Startled for the second time in as many minutes,

all three whipped their heads toward the window, and Bryce was fairly certain he heard a muffled curse escape him as they watched a huge tree outside his office slam to the ground, jarring the entire building.

Pam whimpered just as the lights went out, plunging the room into total darkness.

"Uh, Preacher," Randy said, "I guess this means our session's over."

Bryce silently agreed, realizing this also meant the building-planning committee meeting would have to be postponed, which was too bad since this was the second time it had been called off.

"Reverend Burnette?"

Aware that he was again ignoring the couple, Bryce nudged himself back to the moment at hand. "Why don't you wait to leave? I don't want you out in this weather, not until it calms a bit."

Suddenly the lights flickered, then came back on.

"Oh, thank you, Lord," Pam wheezed, then smiled sheepishly at Bryce as if she'd done something wrong.

"I second that," Bryce said, smiling openly, hoping to ease the tension brought on by the weather as well as their premarital jitters. "If you feel the need to see me again before the big day, I'm here for you."

Bryce paused and swung his chair back toward the window again. "Looks like the worst of the storm has passed, so if you two want to make a run for it, you'd best do it pronto."

A few minutes later Bryce stared at the phone, a frown on his face. He had called Ned Crowley, the maintenance man, and told him about the tree. It hadn't hit anything or anyone; it had just made a big mess.

He'd also called the two members on the committee, and sure enough, they weren't willing to get out in the nasty weather.

Unwittingly Bryce got up and headed for the door. Once there, he paused and stared back at his desk, a feeling of guilt washing over him. Cutting out was not smart. He should stay and go back over the blueprints for the new sanctuary and other refurbishing plans, making sure everything was in perfect order. He also needed to review his sermon for Sunday. But for some reason he felt edgy, out of sorts, and only one person had an antidote for those ills.

With a sigh Bryce closed the door and locked it behind him.

"So how did your meeting go, Son?"

Bryce smiled down at Doris, his sixty-five-year-old mother, who gave him a run for his money when it came to energy and spirit. His smile broadened as his lips grazed across one cheek that barely had a wrinkle on it.

"If you're referring to the committee, it didn't."

"And pray tell why not?"

"The weather."

Doris's clear-blue eyes, a replica of his, stared back at him before cutting to the window. "Why, the sun's shining."

"Well, it wasn't," Bryce countered flatly, "at least

not at the church. The wind uprooted a tree, and when it hit the ground, it barely missed my office.''

"Oh, my goodness," Doris said. "Thank heavens this side of town was spared that.''

"Since it's predicted to come again, I decided to hang it up for the day.''

Doris smiled. "That's obvious, since you're dressed in your sweats.''

"So are you up to having dinner with your son this evening?''

Doris paused, cocking her head to one side. "What's wrong?''

"What makes you think anything's wrong?" Bryce asked, much quicker than he intended.

Doris blatantly ignored the fact that he answered her question with one of his own. "Because I know you. You're in one of your restless moods. Is it the church?''

Bryce didn't respond right off. Instead he sat down in one of the high-backed chairs adjacent to his mother, who sat on the sofa, and perused the room. Like Doris herself it was warm and inviting, filled with expensive yet comfortable furniture, bookcases crammed with books, family pictures and other personal memorabilia.

Adding to the room's warmth was a scattering of live plants, which Doris pampered and petted constantly. Bryce loved this old home almost as much as he loved his mother.

When he had answered the call to become the pastor here in Nacogdoches, his mother had opted to move with him, leaving Houston, her home, where he'd been born and reared.

After his dad died of a heart attack, his mother's heart had begun acting up, though she was fine as long as she took her medication. Still, he hadn't wanted to leave her behind and was relieved and delighted when she'd volunteered to make the transition.

"Your mother asked you a question."

Bryce forced a smile. "Sorry, Mom. I guess I am a bit frustrated because there's been no definite decision on the building plans. You know the Lord didn't bless me with patience."

"Which is something you should work on every day." Doris's tone was scoldingly indulgent.

Bryce's mouth turned down. "I know. I know."

She chuckled, then turned serious. "I have no doubt that you'll eventually get your new sanctuary."

"I'm pretty confident myself, though there is opposition."

"In a church our size, not everyone's going to agree. But then, you know that. For the most part, however, I think the congregation's behind you."

"I guess we'll soon see."

Since his three-year tenure as pastor of this non-denominational church, one of his goals had been to enter a building program. The sanctuary and other parts of the church had been sadly neglected over the years, something that had burdened him.

However, that burden had taken a back seat to a more important concern, and that was lack of attendance. An aggressive drive to entice old members to return plus a search for new ones had paid off. The church had grown and was continuing to grow by leaps and bounds.

And now that his goal was close to becoming a reality, he felt both excited and challenged. Yet he had to be cautious as people were unpredictable, especially when it came to their pocketbooks.

"But it's not the church that's put that glum look on your face." Doris's words were a flat statement of fact and brooked no denial.

Bryce shrugged. "You're right. What I need is to take the plane up for a spin."

One of his joys away from the church was to fly. At age thirty-eight, he'd gotten his pilot's license shortly after he'd arrived, encouraged to do so by a church member who had a private plane. That plane was at Bryce's disposal anytime he chose.

"What you need is a woman."

Bryce's eyes widened.

"Don't look so shocked or offended," Doris retorted. "You know I'm right."

"Now, Mom, don't get on your soapbox again, please."

She gave him a put-out look. "I don't know why I shouldn't. After all, it's been five years since Molly's fatal heart attack. It's time you got on with your life."

"I thought that was what I was doing," Bryce said mildly, shoving his hand through his thick blondish-brown hair.

"Preachers aren't supposed to lie."

"Mother!"

"Don't 'mother' me. You know I'm right."

Her tone was so arrogantly sweet that he couldn't take offense. Still, he felt the need to defend himself. "When I meet the right woman I'll consider remarrying, and not before."

Doris sighed. "How do you propose to meet that woman if you don't go out? If I recall, you just asked your mother to have dinner."

"And what's wrong with that?"

"You're impossible."

Bryce grinned, then sobered. "Look, you know I'm not still grieving over Molly. Time has definitely dulled my pain and my sadness. But the truth of the matter is I haven't found anyone with whom I want a lasting relationship."

"Did you ever consider you're too picky?" She was half smiling.

"Yeah, many times."

"I know someone who'd love to go out with you."

Oh, brother, not again. "Forget it. I'm not interested."

"How do you know? You don't even know who she is."

"And I don't want to. You and your friends forget about fixing me up. It isn't going to happen."

Doris sniffed. "Well, there're a lot of people in the church who'd rather you were married."

"They'll get over it." He grinned, then got up and kissed her cheek again. "Gotta go run some errands, but I'll be back for dinner."

"Are we going out?"

Bryce's eyebrows shot up. "Only if you don't want to cook something for your growing boy."

Doris flapped her hand, then blew him a kiss. "Of course, I'd rather cook. Now, go on, get out of here."

Whistling, Bryce did just that, making his way to the nearest hardware store. He'd been doing slow-but-sure repairs himself on the church parsonage. In order to complete his projects, he needed several specialty tools. Since the weather put a kink in his flying plans, he might as well do manual labor.

He walked through the door at the same time a woman was coming down the aisle in front of him. He pulled up short and stared blatantly at her, something he had never done before, at least not to a stranger.

But then, he hadn't seen anyone in a long time who commanded that kind of attention. With red hair, dark-brown eyes and a perfect body, she sizzled.

And just like that, she pushed his hot button.

Two

Earlier That Day

"**W**ow, this is the best yet!"

Katherine Mays could barely contain her excitement as she continued to pull the lingerie out of the box one item at time.

When her part-time employee, Nancy Holt, didn't answer, she paused, then looked up and gave her a pointed stare. "Don't you agree?"

"They're certainly the sexiest we've ever had."

Katherine pushed a strand of red hair out of her eyes and gave Nancy a crestfallen look. "You don't like them."

Nancy's rather serious face broke into a fleeting

smile. "Of course I like them, silly. It's just that I'm wondering if our customers will."

Katherine grinned. "Some will be horrified, that's for sure. But then some will jump over the moon."

"With as many see-through things as we have here, especially the one you're holding, we'd better hope everyone jumps over that moon."

Katherine's grin grew into an outright laugh. "When they see the display, it ought to be interesting, to say the least."

Nancy sighed then shook her head. "I wish I had just a little of your flare for the dramatic."

"Don't you mean daring?" Katherine quipped.

"Whatever."

Katherine straightened, then winced.

"What's wrong?" Nancy asked.

"I guess I've been hitting the machines too hard at the gym."

"I'd tell you to take it easy, but I'd just be wasting my breath." Nancy took the edge off her words with a smile, though again it didn't last long.

Katherine leaned her head to one side and gave her helper a closer look. Although Nancy was tall and blond and had lovely fair skin, she wasn't a beauty. She did have a flare for style, though, which was the main ingredient needed to work in a boutique.

In addition, she had a sweet demeanor and calmness that made her such an attribute to the shop. But more than those pluses, Nancy was dependable. Katherine didn't want to think about what she would do without her.

Yet this morning there was something different about Nancy, something that Katherine couldn't quite put her finger on. Not only was Nancy's usual enthusiasm missing, but her green eyes were sunken back in her head as if she hadn't slept. Maybe being married to that first-class jerk was finally getting to her.

Katherine grimaced, chiding herself for the uncharitable opinion of Wally Holt. But then "husbands" in general, and Wally in particular, were not high on her priority list.

"Are you all right?" Katherine asked, voicing part of her thoughts.

"I'm okay."

"No, you're not," Katherine countered bluntly.

Nancy sat down in one of the chairs in the back room of the shop that served as an office, a lounge and general catch-all area. "For starters, I didn't sleep at all."

"I'd already guessed that." Katherine walked to the refrigerator, removed a Coke, then poured Nancy about half a glass. "Drink this. Maybe it'll help, though I really think you ought to go home."

A stark look crossed Nancy's features, then she said in a rushed tone, "That's not necessary. I'll be fine."

Katherine watched as she sipped on the Coke and was about to say something else when Nancy jumped to her feet and bolted toward the bathroom.

"Oh, dear," Katherine muttered, hearing retching sounds coming from behind the closed door. Feeling helpless, she finally asked, "Is there anything I can do for you?"

Nancy opened the door, looking as pasty white as the walls on either side of her. "I feel better now," she said.

"Sure coulda fooled me. You're going home."

"No, I—"

"That's an order," Katherine said, her full lower lip tightening. "You probably have a twenty-four-hour bug, so the thing to do is hit the bed and sleep it off."

"All right," Nancy said in a halting tone, though she didn't sound convinced.

"Want me to call Wally and have him come get you?"

"Lord, no," Nancy said. "Besides, he's at work."

"Good, then you'll have the house to yourself and can sleep. Now, get out of here. I'll check on you later."

Once alone, Katherine looked at the clock and noticed it was almost opening time. She had asked Nancy to come in early so they could unbox the merchandise that had arrived late yesterday afternoon.

Her gaze went longingly to the three other boxes that were filled with party dresses, costume jewelry and more lingerie. The goodies inside would have to remain there at least for another day or maybe more. She couldn't work in the back and up front, too.

Nancy's bout with her stomach couldn't have come at a worse time. Katherine rubbed the back of her neck, giving in to that niggling feeling that all was not well in the Holt household. But again, if Nancy wasn't willing to confide in her, there wasn't anything she could do.

Katherine fingered the gauzy negligee one last time before tossing it aside. She then headed toward the front where she turned the sign around, though it was still ten minutes before she had officially to open.

That done, she headed toward the counter only to change direction as she saw a couple of dresses hanging askew on a rack. After straightening them, she surveyed the entire premises. And smiled a giddy smile.

Katherine's.

Hers. Hers and the bank's, she modified silently. Someday she would get the note paid off, something she longed to do so that she could open another shop in a small town nearby.

Katherine's Two. She already had the name picked out. But that goal would have to wait, as her cash flow was not what it could be after just two years in business. However, her accountant and advisor assured her that she was on target and to be patient, a virtue that heretofore remained elusive.

The jingling of the phone forced her to move. It was Dave Morehead, a man she'd been dating.

"Hey, what's up?" she asked.

"Just confirming our date for tomorrow night."

"Are we still going dancing?"

"You bet," he said in his gruff voice.

Dave was a young, overweight cowboy, who, true to his roots, loved country-western music. And despite the fact that he was a big man, he was quick and light on his feet. While that wasn't her favorite music, she loved to dance, no matter the music.

"How 'bout dinner first?" he asked, breaking into her thoughts. "At my place?"

A warning bell went off in her head. Dave was okay for a dance partner, but that was as far as it would ever go. He was a friend and that was all he'd ever be, especially since he was carrying more baggage than she was. He had an ex-wife who gave him hell and three children to boot. No way would she get involved with the likes of him. He was just one in a long list of many that she dated.

"Let's skip the dinner and stick to the dancing," she said at last.

He didn't seem to take offense. "No problem. I'll pick you up at eight."

Dismissing him from her mind, her hand remained on the phone. She was tempted to call her best friend Lee Ann James and see if she was available to come in and help. But that thought died a natural death. Lee Ann had her own interior design business to run. Though she was certainly flexible, she had a rather hectic agenda at times, and this was probably one of those times, Katherine told herself.

Besides, it would do her good to work the front for a change. She hadn't mingled with or visited with her customers on a one-on-one basis in quite a while.

If there was a downside to this business, it was the paperwork. It was a killer and took up an immense amount of her time, time she often resented.

However, that resentment didn't last long. She couldn't think of anything else she would rather do or any place she'd rather be than here in this sleepy town in the heart of the piney woods, the place she'd always called home.

After graduating from college with a degree in merchandising and design, she'd married a wealthy congressman. Because she had wanted to make a success of her marriage, she had forfeited her own career and tried to become what he wanted her to be, a decision that proved to have been disastrous.

Hence her marriage had failed and a nasty divorce had followed. Behind that were several unsatisfactory jobs. That was when she decided to return to her roots, though minus her family. Her parents were long gone, having divorced when she was young. Both had remarried and were the proud parents of other children, a fact she had never resented.

Thankfully, Katherine had been reared by her grandmother, a wonderful lady, who had loved her and given her a strong sense of values. Gram had died peacefully in her sleep several years ago, and she still missed her.

Now, at thirty, two years after opening the shop, Katherine had finally found contentment in her life, if not happiness. She loved her work, and when the opportunity presented itself, she enjoyed traveling.

Her days were full and so were her nights, crammed with men friends who loved to have a good time and who came with no strings attached.

She was once more in control of her life, and she vowed never to lose that control again.

"Hey, it's sure good to see you."

So lost in thought was Katherine that she hadn't even heard the buzzer on the door. She grinned at Lucy Rivers, one of her oldest and steadiest customers.

"Same here," Katherine said, meeting her in the middle of the shop and giving her a hug. "So how are things?"

"They'll be great if you can find me the sexiest and skimpiest thing you have. Today's Mike's and my tenth wedding anniversary."

Katherine's eyes flared and she grinned, grabbing Lucy by the arm. "Oh, honey, have I got just the thing for you."

She flipped the sign to Closed, then locked the door.

Whew, what a day. One customer after another had followed Lucy, and the day's receipts were bound to reflect the amount of traffic she'd had. And she wasn't even running a sale.

She'd done it all on her own, which added to her goodwill. But she hadn't forgotten about her co-worker. She'd called Nancy twice and was assured both times that she was okay and to expect her back at work the next day.

No complaints from her end, though she was dog tired, too tired to go to the gym. What she did have to do, however, was make a quick trip across the strip mall to the hardware store to buy a new faucet, something the landlord had promised to do yet hadn't.

That afternoon the one in the bathroom had crashed and burned. It wouldn't even turn on, thus no water. She couldn't install it, but she could at least have one on hand that *she'd* chosen when the plumber showed up.

The hardware store was empty of customers, except for one man. Later Katherine had no idea why she even noticed him. Maybe it was because he was staring at her. But that was no big deal, as she was used to being stared at. If nothing else, her coloring commanded that kind of attention.

She nodded briefly, then dismissed him, spotting the aisle with the faucets and making her way there. It was only after she was fuming over the fact that she had failed to measure the size of the existing faucet that she became aware of him again. He was perusing the rack next to her.

"Maybe I could help you," he said as if sensing her frustration.

God, what a voice. She swung around and stared at him, brown eyes colliding with blue ones.

Three

Most people couldn't expect to have more standout traits than a great voice and vivid-blue eyes. Not so with this man. Those assets were just the tip of the iceberg.

He had a face to die for. And a body that certainly didn't play second fiddle. With him, one seemed to go along with the other—a packaged deal.

Realizing she was staring like a kid turned loose in a candy store, Katherine averted her gaze, though reluctantly.

The truth was, she'd been married to a man who was just as physically endowed. Unfortunately, that was the only thing Jack Forrest had going for him.

Suddenly she frowned. Rarely did she think about

her ex-husband. But every once in a while, thoughts of him would hit her unexpectedly, which never failed to darken her mood.

"You really *must* be having trouble."

That voice again. Still the best. Even better than the rest of him. She hadn't decided if it sounded more like the richest of cream or the smoothest of liquor.

Jerking herself out of candyland, she eased her head toward him. Again their eyes met, but just for the briefest of moments. However, that was enough to elevate her heart rate.

"Do you work here?" she asked, hoping that he didn't. A hardware salesman? Uh-uh.

He smiled. "Actually, I don't."

She barely heard his words. This time it was his smile that worked on her heart rate. He had perfect lips, too. And tanned skin that served as a backdrop for straight, white teeth.

"So how can you help me?" she asked bluntly, though a smile toyed with her lips.

His smile was sheepish. "I probably can't, since I'm having trouble myself."

He had thick, dark-blond hair and muscles galore, though not too bulked up. She had been in enough gyms to know that underneath his sweats was yet another hotbed of perfection.

Lot of good all that eye candy would do for her. She was certain that he was taken. The good ones usually were. Under thick eyelashes her eyes slid to his left hand. No ring. But that didn't mean anything. Jack had opted not to wear a wedding band.

"I can't find what I'm looking for, either," he stressed, breaking into the silence. "I'm not sure I even know."

"Well, I know, but I didn't do my homework."

One eyebrow raised. "How so?"

She told him about the faucet.

"Don't be too hard on yourself," he remarked. "Plumbing skills aren't supposed to be a 'woman thing.'"

Her lips twitched even harder. "And what exactly is a 'woman thing'?"

"Whoa." He chuckled and held up his hand. "I'm not about to go there."

"I would hope not," she said, giving him a challenging look.

For another long second their gazes met and held.

Katherine flushed and was the first to turn away, feeling more foolish than ever. It had been a long time since she'd outright flirted with a man and enjoyed the heck out of it.

Unfortunately, all good things must come to an end. Besides, he could be some kind of pervert who prayed on innocent women, and in a hardware store, no less. She almost laughed out loud again at the absurdity of such a thought.

"Well, good luck," he said.

Katherine nodded. "Same to you."

She watched as he walked off, especially the swagger of his tight butt. Swallowing a sigh for what might have been, she stared at the row after row of faucets, then threw up her hands in silent frustration.

"Ma'am, do you need any help?"

She faced a thin, pimple-faced young man with an earring in his right earlobe. "Not now. I'll have to come back."

He merely nodded, then strode away. Katherine did the same thing, only to remember suddenly that she was going out that evening. She almost stopped in her tracks, wondering why that thought was so unappetizing.

She knew. Thoughts of that piece of live artwork in motion she'd just seen and talked to came back to mind. It was a crying shame she'd never see him again. Or better yet, maybe they would meet another time in the hardware store. Stranger things had happened.

Crazy! Katherine chuckled, then shook her head.

"So, gentlemen, what are you thinking?"

Bryce stared at two members of his congregation, members who were also friends. At the same time he pushed his chair back from his desk, narrowing his eyes.

Pete Hanover, the chairman of the building committee, stared at him through glasses that rested under a thick shelf of dark brows. "I think it'll be a definite go."

"I second that," Tucker Gaston added, shifting his well-toned body in the chair while rubbing his balding head.

"You've done an excellent job of making a clear plan for the new sanctuary as well as the other refurbishing projects," Pete said, "without all the extravagance that usually accompanies such an undertaking. What more could the church body ask for?"

Bryce knew he could count on the men for their support. Not only were they influential in the church, but in the community, as well. Both had money—megabucks, in fact. Pete was a rancher, while Tucker had investments in several lucrative businesses including the stock market, having inherited oil money from his dad.

Neither was pretentious, however, especially Tucker who was his best friend, along with his wife Trish. They had stood by him through the good times and the bad here at the church, even though they hadn't always agreed with him. In addition, it was Tucker's plane that he flew whenever he wanted to.

"I appreciate that vote of confidence, but I can't take the credit," Bryce said at last. "You and the other committee members more than did your part."

"Still," Tucker said, "you're the one who's been spearheading the endeavor, and like Pete pointed out, it's a package that I think we can all live with."

"All we need now," Pete said, "is to bring it before the church and vote on it."

Bryce leaned forward in his chair, barely able to contain his excitement. This moment was the one he'd been waiting for from the get-go. Once he'd learned the growth potential of this church, he had known in his heart that it was the Divine's will that His people have a new and beautiful place to worship.

If it didn't go over—no, he wouldn't think about that. He would think positive.

"When it passes," Bryce said with renewed confidence, "then we'll be faced with a drive to raise the money to pay for it."

"I know how you feel about us being in so much debt, but we can handle that, too. When this congregation makes a commitment, you'll see how firmly we dig our heels in to make it work."

Bryce smiled. "Well, I for one can't wait."

Tucker answered his smile. "So let's do it. Let's get the ballots printed and our presentation perfected, then bring it before the membership. I see no point in waiting any longer."

"As soon as the vote's taken and passed," Pete said, "there's no reason we can't get started at least on the refurbishing part, using the money we have in savings."

Bryce voiced a silent prayer of thanksgiving for this meeting and what had come out of it. The only sad part was that he didn't have anyone to share his innermost feelings with. If Molly was alive, he would snap up the phone and call her. But Molly wasn't here and that was that.

Life had to go on, and it had. As he'd told his mother, he was open to falling in love again, when and if he found the right woman. And he was adamant that she be someone just like Molly, who had the same commitment to church work as he had.

Suddenly his thoughts shifted to the redhead in the hardware store, only then to feel his stomach bottom out. He didn't know why—he didn't want to delve that deeply—but he knew she was no Molly. He had no idea what she was committed to, but he'd bet it wasn't church related.

"Bryce."

"Uh, sorry Tuck," Bryce said, reeling his thoughts back to where they belonged. "I guess I was just woolgathering."

Tucker rubbed his bald head again as he chuckled. "You're entitled."

"I'm assuming we're done here," Pete said, uncoiling his tall frame and standing. "I gotta run. My cows are calling."

Bryce, along with Tucker, also stood. But it was Bryce who spoke first, smiling. "Then you'd best head 'em out. Can't let your prize cattle want for a thing."

Pete shook hands with both men, then walked out. Tucker turned back to Bryce and said, "Are you on for some lunch?"

"I was thinking about taking the plane up instead."

Tucker removed a pipe from his pocket as he gave Bryce an indulgent look. "When it comes to that plane, you're like a kid with a new toy."

"And thanks to you and your generosity, I get to play with that toy anytime I want."

"You got *that* right."

"But I keep telling you not to let me abuse the privilege, though I'm not sure you're listening."

Tucker gave him a frustrated look. "It's my private plane, not associated with the company at all. And as you know, I don't fly much anymore. When I'm not working, Trish and the girls keep me busy. So enough said, okay?''

"Okay, good buddy, I won't belabor the point."

"Good. Go take her for a spin, and I'll talk to you later."

"Thanks again."

Tucker paused at the door. "Hey, afterward, why don't you come to dinner? We haven't had the pleasure of your company in a while."

"Have you cleared this invitation with your better half?"

Tucker shrugged. "You're not company, so it doesn't matter."

"You have a date, but if she whips up on you, I refuse to take your side."

"I hear you," Tucker said, grinning, then walked out the door.

Thirty minutes later Bryce was flying high, literally. Following the storm that had blown through a few days before, the air was cool and crystal clear. And not a cloud in the sky, he noticed as he gazed all about him.

What a feeling. Flying always gave him the sensation of floating. Nothing could compare with it except maybe having sex. He jerked the controls, and when he did, the plane took a nosedive.

Once he had things back under control, he realized his heart was hammering in his chest.

Sex.

Now where had that thought come from?

A groan split his lips. That redhead. For some ludicrous reason he associated her with sex. Maybe it was because her very presence had transmitted sexual signals. He knew there were women who were capable of that, but he'd never encountered one. Not until her, that is.

So what was the deal?

There was no deal. She was just a beautiful, sexy woman he'd met by accident in a local store. He squirmed in the seat, knowing he was lying to himself, something he tried never to do.

With him a spade was a spade, and he prided himself on calling it that way. However, sex was the last thing he should have on his mind, especially since he had no one special in his life.

Bryce's fingers tightened around the controls as he tried to get his mind off her. But his brain refused to cooperate, along with something else.

He took a deep breath, then blew it out. Still, her face remained in front of his. When she'd walked into that store flaunting her great body, that flame-red hair framing her beautiful face, it had had the same effect as lighting a match in a room filled with gasoline.

His insides had exploded. Even now he was experiencing that same feeling again.

Suddenly he couldn't stand the solitude of being alone. He had to return to earth in more ways than one.

He veered, then headed the plane toward home, all the while praying out loud, ''Lord, still my anxious heart back to calm delight.''

Four

"**W**hew, I'm beat." Katherine looked over at Nancy. "And, Lordy, my feet, they'll never be the same." Even as she moaned those words, she kicked her heels off and plopped down in the nearest chair.

"I'm tired, too," Nancy admitted, "though not on your level. After all, I didn't do that much of the work."

"Pooh, you did plenty." Katherine stared closely at her cohort, who seemed to have fully recovered from her bout with the virus. But there was still something not quite right about Nancy.

Again, until Nancy decided to confide in her, she had no choice but to keep her mouth shut.

"I think this particular trunk show went great,"

Nancy was saying, having walked to the refrigerator in the office and taken out a Coke. When she faced Katherine again, she added, "In fact, I think it might've been our best."

"Well, that particular bridge group that meets at the club is not only huge, but they love to spend money."

Nancy smiled, and for a moment Katherine saw the old Nancy, which made her wonder if she had imagined those shadows in her eyes.

"Especially on pretty things from your shop."

Katherine smiled and reached for her share of the beverage that Nancy poured her. "We aim to please. But the proof's in the pudding, right? So let's see if they put their money where their mouths are."

"They will," Nancy said with calm confidence. "You just wait and see."

"Meanwhile, we have to unpack the rest of those boxes in addition to the other two that have since arrived."

This time Nancy moaned. "Slave driver."

Katherine feigned shock. "Why, you wouldn't have it any other way."

Nancy gulped down a healthy swig of Coke, then stood. "You're right, I wouldn't. So I guess I might as well get started."

Katherine gave her an incredulous stare. "Hey, I didn't mean now, not even today."

"Why not?" Nancy asked innocently, shoving some strands of her long blond hair behind one ear.

"That should be obvious. Even discounting the day we've had, it's after closing time."

"So?"

"So what about Wally?"

Nancy shrugged and averted her gaze. "He'll be all right."

"The kids won't."

"They're with my mother."

"Well, go home anyway, my friend. *I'm* going home. Even if you don't have to cater to your family, cater to yourself. Take a long, soaking bath."

Nancy sighed on a grin. "Sounds like heaven."

"Then do it."

Nancy saluted. "Yes, ma'am."

"See you tomorrow."

Not long after Nancy left, Katherine was in the process of locking up when the phone rang. She paused, undecided if she should answer it or not. It was probably a customer wanting to know if they could exchange an item after she'd already worn it.

Swallowing an exasperated sigh, she dropped her belongings on the spot and hurried to the counter. It was her best friend, Lee Ann James.

"Hey, what's up?"

"Dinner."

"Now?" Katherine asked.

Lee Ann laughed. "Why not? It's the dinner hour. Am I not correct?"

"Smarty."

"I'll pick you up."

"Hey, hold on," Katherine said. "Why don't you

come to the house? I have some fresh turkey and bread from the deli, as well as fruit.''

''Are you sure you want to eat at home?''

''How can you ask that after the day I've had? You were there.''

Lee Ann made a sound. ''That's why I'm asking you out to dinner, my friend.''

''I'll meet you at the house.''

Katherine walked inside her home and immediately felt the tiredness evaporate. It was a small two-bedroom, two-bath that she'd bought and remodeled. The one thing that made it unique was the loft that was part bedroom and part library. The times she'd had overnight guests, they never seemed to want to go home, which was proof that she had done something right.

As she dropped her things in the nearest chair, the faint aroma from the fireplace still permeated the air. She had burned it that morning while she'd had her coffee. She had almost replaced the real thing with gas logs, but changed her mind. Even though the fireplace was messy more often than not, she preferred the ambiance of the real McCoy.

Katherine shivered from the chill in the air and instantly reset the thermostat. She cut her eyes toward the bathroom and gazed longingly at her deep tub, which she envisioned filled with sweet-smelling bubbles.

Later. Once Lee Ann was gone, she'd indulge. As if on cue the doorbell pealed and the door opened.

"Yo, anybody home?"

"I'm in the bedroom," Katherine called, "ditching these dang panty hose."

"Lord, there's no relief like it. You'll be a new woman."

Katherine was chuckling as she came out of the room and faced her friend. Lee Ann was one of a kind, both in looks and temperament. She had black hair and black eyes that were always sparkling. Even though she was short and plump, she was full of energy. How she managed her husband, her toddler daughter, Mitzy, and ran her interior design business with such laid-back ease never failed to amaze Katherine.

Lee Ann was like a soft, gentle breeze while she, Katherine, was like the shifting winds of a storm. Yet they were firm friends and had been since childhood. If it hadn't been for Lee Ann's help and encouragement, she never would've opened Katherine's.

"Would you like something to drink before we chow down?" Katherine asked, giving Lee Ann a quick hug.

"A glass of wine would be nice."

"You're a lady after my own heart."

Once the wine was poured and they were seated on either end of the sofa, knees drawn up, looking like unmatched bookends, they sipped quietly on the wine.

Lee Ann was the first to break the silence. "You can't imagine how relaxing this is."

"How did you manage to get an evening away from Josh and Mitzy?"

"They're at Josh's mother's. I thought they needed the time with her alone." Lee Ann smiled. "You know that bonding thing."

"Yeah, right."

"So, anything going on with you I need to know about?"

"Okay, nosy," Katherine said in a teasing voice, "I went dancing with Dave the other night."

Lee Ann rolled her eyes. "That overweight manure kicker? Why do you waste your time with him?"

"That's not nice. Besides, he's a great guy."

"For someone else," Lee Ann countered with her mouth turned down.

"Well, I'm not in the market for anyone with sticking power, so he suits me just fine."

"Even if Mr. Right came along and pinched you on the butt, you wouldn't be interested?"

"Not if it means a ring and the rest of the trimmings."

Lee Ann merely shook her head.

Katherine got up and headed toward the kitchen. "Come on, let's grab something to eat before I pass out."

A while later they were back on the sofa with another glass of wine in hand and watching the logs glow in the fireplace.

"I've been thinking," Lee Ann said at last, setting her glass down and giving Katherine a pointed stare.

"Oh, brother. When you 'think' with that look on your face, it usually means trouble."

"That's a low blow."

''That's the truth.''

Lee Ann popped her playfully on the leg. ''You really ought to get back in church.''

''What?'' Katherine asked, not bothering to hide her shock.

''You sound like I've just asked you to have a root canal when you didn't need one.''

Katherine gave her head a vigorous shake. ''That's pretty much how I feel.''

''You're awful.''

''Why all of a sudden do you want me to attend church?''

''I need a favor, but that's not the only reason I want you back in the fold.''

''If the favor is church related, count me out.''

''Hey, don't go ballistic on me yet,'' Lee Ann pleaded. ''At least wait until I've made my pitch.''

''Give it your best shot,'' Katherine said, her tone unyielding.

''Our church is about to vote to build a new sanctuary along with approving other cosmetic surgery for the staff offices and parlor.''

''Wonderful.''

Lee Ann ignored her sarcasm and went on, ''I'm in charge of the decorating committee, and I desperately need your help.''

''Pray tell why?'' Katherine grinned. ''No pun intended.''

''Sure.''

''Look, you have lots of capable women to choose from. You don't need me. It's just an excuse to get me back in church.'' Katherine raised a perfectly arched brow. "And I'm not about to fall for it.''

"I really do need your help.'' Lee Ann's tone was desperate. "The biddies who would volunteer wouldn't know style and design if it bit them through their hide-tight girdles.''

Katherine laughed. "Well, get some young ones then.''

"You know it doesn't work that way. Politics, my dear. So please, take pity and help me.''

Katherine wanted to scream, "Absolutely not,'' but she didn't because guilt gave her sudden lockjaw. Lee Ann was always doing special things for her, mainly touting her shop and sending her customers who had megabucks.

"All right,'' she conceded, "I'll help, but I won't become active in church.''

Lee Ann held up her hand. "I understand. I know you had a bad experience when you were married to Jack, and it still smarts.''

"That it does.''

"At least go this Sunday so you can get a feel of what the church is about and see what it looks like now.''

"What if the building project doesn't pass?''

"It will,'' Lee Ann said loftily.

"As long as you don't start preaching to me,'' Katherine said with forced humor.

"Ah, speaking of preaching, even if you don't like what our pastor says, you'll sure like how he looks.''

"Don't start. Preachers are like politicians. They

are owned by the people they serve. I've been there, done that.''

''You just wait. You'll see.''

The church pews were crowded, and there seemed to be excitement in the air. Still, Katherine wished she were anywhere but here.

Lee Ann, sitting next to her, gave her a nudge. ''So what do you think?''

''About what?''

''You know.''

''No, I don't.''

''Being back in the Lord's house after so long?''

''Lee Ann, you promised,'' Katherine pointed out, feeling uncomfortable, as if she was on the proverbial hot seat and didn't know why. No one was looking at her. Oh, several members had welcomed her, spotting her as a visitor.

During her church-going days, she and Jack had attended a Baptist church in Ft. Worth. She felt her face wrinkle in a frown, and she hated that. Suddenly she felt the urge to get up and bolt. Instead she took a deep breath and told herself to behave, that attending one church service was a nothingburger.

Still, she felt that Lee Ann had conned her, taken unfair advantage. But again she would live through it as it was a one-time deal.

The organ belting out the song ''Onward Christian Soldiers'' claimed her attention, which was good. The music was followed by the side door opening and two men walking in. Only one, however, stepped up to the pulpit.

Her breath caught in her throat.

It couldn't be. Surely that gorgeous hunk in the hardware store wasn't...

Lee Ann nudged her again, shattering her thoughts. "That's our minister, Bryce Burnette," she whispered.

A preacher. She still couldn't believe it. She didn't want to believe it. What a waste of manhood.

Five

It was her.

Sweat burst out on Bryce's upper lip. In fact, sweat dampened his entire body.

At first he was sure it had been a case of mistaken identity or that he had imagined that drop-dead gorgeous redhead sitting in his church, in the middle pew, right in his line of vision.

He'd blinked several times. Nothing changed. He hadn't been mistaken; he was dead on target. She indeed the same woman he'd talked to in the hardware store, the same woman who'd been haunting him since.

Suddenly their eyes met, and all the oxygen seemed to have been sucked out of the room. He strove to regain control of himself and the situation. But that was difficult, as he was terribly disconcerted at having her in his congregation, a feeling that had never happened to him in all of his ministry.

Why now?

Was God telling him something? If so, what? He fought the urge to dig into his rear pocket and pull out his handkerchief and mop his face. Wonder what his worshipers would think about that? More to the point, what would they think if they could read his thoughts?

He lifted his eyes. God had to help him. Apparently, he couldn't help himself.

Somehow Bryce managed to say what he had to say, then sit down. The associate minister, who also led the music, followed him. Still, Bryce couldn't seem to pull himself together or take his eyes off her. He figured no one else was aware of his fixation, especially with the hymnal in front of his face, even though he knew the song by heart.

What if? Nah. He hadn't lost his composure to that extent. Yet he checked, only to let out a sigh of relief. His hymnal wasn't upside down, after all.

For a moment he felt the urge to laugh out loud, but he quelled that urge, continuing to belt out the words of the song, convinced his face was as red as the red in his tie.

Who was she? What was she doing at his church? Was she a visitor? Or was she a member who simply didn't attend? Those questions rattled around inside his head, intensifying the sweat on his upper lip. Realizing he couldn't get back up to the pulpit sweating like a field hand, he finally gave in and reached for his handkerchief.

He wondered if she would get in line after the service to shake his hand. Suddenly disgusted with his uncharacteristic lack of self-discipline, he forced his mind off her and onto the sermon he was soon to deliver. When he stepped up to the pulpit again, he made sure he looked elsewhere.

"Please open your Bibles and follow along as I read the morning's scriptures."

Two hours later Bryce was alone in his office. He had turned down five luncheon invitations, one of them from his mother, who proceeded to lecture him on the spot.

"Why aren't you hungry?"

"Now, Mom, don't nag."

"Of course I'll nag," she said without hesitation. "That's what mothers are supposed to do when their children are out of line."

He leaned over and kissed her on the cheek, then smiled with as much good-humored tolerance as he could muster. "I'm hardly a child, and I'm not hungry."

"Since when?"

"Since right now," he countered, hanging on to his patience. "I'll grab a bite a little later. I promise."

She brushed his cheek with the back of her hand, frowning. "Are you sure something's not bothering you?'' Her white brows were drawn together. ''You look—''

''Fine, which is exactly how I am.''

''All right,'' she finally conceded, ''I'll leave you be, but call me later.''

''Will do.''

Now, as he sat behind his desk with paperwork strewn across it, he couldn't concentrate, except on *her*. If it hadn't been such a ludicrous thought, he would declare he'd become possessed.

Bryce lunged to his feet and shoved a hand through his hair. She hadn't gotten in line to greet him. Disappointment. At the moment that was the emotion charging through him, making him as jumpy as a stalked deer.

Why had that particular woman, a woman whose name he didn't even know, for heaven's sake, have his stomach tied in knots? That had never happened to him before, not even with Molly, and he didn't have a clue how to deal with it.

Yes, he did.

Forget his libido and get his thoughts back on track, back on his work, the Lord's work, to be exact. Most likely he would never see her again, and if he did, he'd surely realize that he'd blown her and everything connected with her out of proportion.

But what if she was a potential member? If she were any other visitor, he wouldn't ignore her. He'd find out who she was, which would be easy enough to do.

She had been with Lee Ann James. If he were willing to cave in to his emotions, all he had to do was pick up the phone and make a call. Voilà! The mystery of the redhead would be solved.

He stared at the phone. He was tempted. He placed his hand on the receiver. No. He couldn't do it, reminding himself that he would be contacting her for all the wrong reasons.

Besides, she wasn't for him. On the best of days, she was way of out his league. Yet he couldn't seem to remove his hand from the phone. Should he call?

"Am I interrupting?"

Bryce gave a start. The associate pastor stood in the doorway. He was short and wiry with a mustache that covered all the space between his upper lip and nose.

"Of course not," Bryce said, motioning him toward one of the chairs in front of his desk. "What's on your mind?"

"Rumblings."

"About the upcoming vote?"

Travis nodded.

Bryce merely smiled. "You didn't expect that?"

"Not to such an extent," Travis said, his voice troubled. "I thought we were pretty much united in this effort."

Bryce smothered his sigh. "Suppose you tell me exactly what you heard and from whom."

The day was bright and crisp.

When Katherine unlocked the door, she pushed it open and breathed deeply. Her eyes went to the sky, where there wasn't a cloud to be seen. The sun shone like a huge yellow diamond.

Days like this were rare in East Texas. For the most part, September was still considered summer and usually hotter than blue blazes. But this year a cool front had blown in early and knocked the temperature for a loop, which was just fine with her.

Maybe now the shop would sell even more of its fall and winter party dresses, get everyone in the holiday spirit early.

She was smiling to herself when she strode back in, ready for her first customer. Nancy was coming in later, as one of her boys had high fever and she was taking him to the doctor.

Katherine had wanted to ask why Wally couldn't have assumed that responsibility since he was on his five days off, but she had kept her mouth shut. After all, Nancy had the time coming.

Finally all the boxes were unpacked, the merchandise marked and in place under the counters and on the racks. However, any order would be short-lived. The next shipment would nix that.

Katherine flinched at that thought, then made her way to the bathroom, where her eyes instantly went to the new faucet that had recently been installed.

She wondered if the Reverend Bryce Burnette ever found what he was looking for. Her mind rebelled. *Not him again.* The last person she wanted to think about on such a perfect day was that preacher, even if he was about the best-looking specimen she'd seen in a long time.

A minister.

Her mind still reeled from the fact. When he'd walked up to that pulpit and she'd realized who her fantasy man really was, her stomach had hollowed out with regret. That feeling hadn't gone away, even though she'd gotten over the shock.

Well, sort of. The casually dressed man she'd talked to in the hardware store had borne very little semblance to the man behind the podium who had been dressed to the nines.

Even now, when she thought about the way he'd filled out that suit and the special smile he'd given the congregation, her insides fluttered, a fact she'd like to ignore but couldn't.

She would, though. She had given her word to Lee Ann, to help with the decorating. But when it came to Bryce Burnette specifically, she would steer clear of him. But it wasn't just Bryce. It was ministers and churches in general.

One of her most hurtful moments had come from a minister while she'd been married to Jack. They had attended a Baptist church in Ft. Worth when Jack's schedule as a politician would allow it.

She'd gone to Dr. Bell for counseling after cracks in her marriage started developing.

"I can't seem to reach my husband any longer," she'd told him without mincing words. "He's suddenly become jealous and possessive." She paused and struggled for her next breath. Unburdening herself like this was so hard, much harder than she'd thought it would be. "He even accused me of seeing another man, of having an affair."

"Are you? Seeing another man, I mean?"

Katherine was shocked. "Of course not."

"I'm sorry if you took that wrong, but I had to ask. You see, I've known Jack Forrest all his life and—"

Suddenly Katherine stood, her heart pounding out of her chest. "And he would never lie. Is that what you were going to say?"

This time it was the minister who looked shocked. "Yes, but—"

Again she interrupted. "Look, it's quite obvious whose side you're on regardless of the facts."

He stood as well. "Please, you're upsetting yourself for no reason. Certainly I want to hear what you have to say."

"Oh, really. You couldn't have proved that by me." She knew she was being rude and probably overreacting, but he was at fault, as well. He was pious at best and condescending at worst. For both, she ached to slap his face.

As if he could read her mind, the lines on Dr. Bell's face flooded with color, and he had the sensitivity at least to appear repentant. "It wasn't my intention to offend you. It's just that Jack Forrest—" He paused and cleared his throat as if again searching for the right words that would dig him out the hole he'd fallen into.

"Gives megabucks to the church," she said, finishing the sentence for him. "And no way are you going to think or say ill of him."

"You're putting words in my mouth, my dear," he said, his color deepening. "Please sit back down and let's start over again."

"I don't think so."

With that she had turned around and walked out. Since then she hadn't been back to church. Just thinking about that episode still made her blood boil.

Organized religion was not for her and never would be again.

Katherine heard the buzzer and hurried out to the front only to stop dead in her tracks.

"Good morning. I was beginning to think no one was here."

It was him. In the flesh. In her store. Staring at her through those incredible eyes.

Damn!

Six

"**G**ood morning back," Katherine finally managed to get out around that old fluttering sensation in her stomach that both infuriated and excited her.

He chuckled, then shot out his hand. "Don't you think it's time we were formally introduced."

No, she wanted to say, but didn't. For one thing, a part of her was glad that he was here while another was not. Neither made any sense.

"Of course I already know who you are." She took his outstretched hand, though only briefly. Even at that her skin felt scorched where it had rested against his.

Katherine sucked in her breath and noticed he, too, seemed to be having trouble breathing as their eyes met and held.

Bryce cleared his throat, then stepped back. However, his "turn on" smile never wavered or faded. "And I know who you are."

Her eyes widened slightly. "Oh, really?"

"Lee Ann told me."

"Figures."

"She didn't volunteer the info. I asked her."

Katherine strove for a casual tone. "That's interesting." She realized that was an idiotic thing to say, but he was flustering her to no end. She wasn't used to being tongue-tied around a man. Nor was she used to her face turning the color of her hair.

"She only told me your name, however."

Katherine found that hard to believe, but was relieved. On more occasions than not, Lee Ann was known to be a blabbermouth.

"Oh, and she said that you were her best friend."

"I feel the same about her. I can't remember when we weren't friends." Apparently Lee Ann could be discreet when she wanted to, having chosen not to mention the fact that Katherine had agreed to be a part of the decorating committee. But then the church hadn't voted on the building package, so it might not come about.

"I was glad to see you in church last Sunday," he said, filling another silence.

"Lee Ann can be persuasive."

"Then I guess she has another thanks coming."

Katherine felt her color deepening, along with his stare. Her skin prickled with a renewed awareness she didn't want to admit. Disgusting. That was what her reaction to him was. She had to stop this nonsense. But there was something about him that made her take on a new personality, especially when it was obvious he was close to flirting with her.

"Uh, that's a nice thing to say."

He chuckled again.

Tread softly, girl, she warned herself. This man could be detrimental to her health in more ways than one. If only he weren't a minister, she'd be giving as good as she was getting. But he *was* a minister, who owed his soul and life to God and the people he served.

"Do you mind if I look around?"

"Of course not," Katherine said at last, realizing the silence had built to a high tension. "Help yourself, though I can't think of why."

"Why I'd like to look around?" he asked.

His lips were twitching, which heightened his attraction. She forced herself to look away. Enough was enough.

"Is that what you meant?" he pressed, when she failed to answer.

"Exactly."

"Curiosity, for one thing."

Well, at least he was honest. But of course he was honest, she told herself, mentally kicking her backside. He was a preacher, for mercy's sake.

"You have my permission to satisfy your curiosity all you want."

"Thank you, ma'am," he said in a slow, mocking drawl.

He was making fun, no doubt, but she didn't take offense. He did it in such a mild-mannered and charming way that she couldn't take offense. But she wanted to. She wanted to find something that was repulsive about him, something that was a total turn-off.

Zilch.

He had on a yellow long-sleeved shirt, open at the neck, which allowed her to see a faint sprinkling of crisp hair. A casual pair of tan slacks hugged his long legs to perfection. Added to the perfection was the aroma of his cologne, not too much, but just enough that it tantalized her senses at odd moments.

Damn, she thought, her hormones were threatening to go haywire on her again. The sooner he satisfied his curiosity, or whatever had brought him there, and left, the better off she would be.

"Actually I'm more than curious."

Her eyebrows arched, but she didn't respond verbally.

"I need a gift for someone special."

So he had a woman. She should've been praising the Lord for that fact. Instead, she felt as if someone had just sucker punched her.

"Like what?" she asked, forcing an aloof calmness into her voice that she was far from feeling. If he had her pick out some piece of flimsy negligee, she would croak.

He smiled that same warm smile. "Perhaps a piece of costume jewelry. I hardly think any of your other merchandise would do."

His tone wasn't critical, just matter-of-fact, which rattled *her* curiosity cage. What kind of woman wouldn't like party dresses and negligees? A prude, that's who, someone who would be married to a preacher. Somehow that type of woman didn't fit him. She suspected he just might enjoy an intense roll in the hay.

Suddenly her face felt torched again, and she had to turn away for fear that he could read her torrid and forbidden thoughts.

"Here's what I have to offer." She pointed toward the jewelry case.

"The gift's for my mother," he said, finally looking up from the sundry pins, earrings and necklaces twinkling at him from under the glass.

Sudden relief washed through Katherine, which made her kick her backside again, but for a different reason. This was crazy! *She was crazy.*

"See anything you think she'd like?" Katherine asked, thinking at least her voice sounded normal.

"That pin." He pointed to a small flower, the petals made from yellow cubic zircons.

She smiled. "Good choice. That's one of my favorites."

"Do you gift wrap?" he asked, scrutinizing her closely.

Katherine squirmed inwardly under that scrutiny, but she wasn't about to let him know that. Cool. Keep your cool. He would be out of here shortly, and life as she once knew it would go on. That absurd thought brought a smile.

"I like that."

"What?" she asked inanely.

"Your smile. It's infectious."

"Uh, thanks," she said, swallowing with difficulty.

He gave a knowing smile as if he sensed he'd made her uncomfortable. "You're welcome."

"I'll have this wrapped in a jiffy," she said, dashing to the back where she fought to get her breath and hold her hands steady enough to wrap the pin.

She had never reacted to a man this way in her entire life, not even when she first met Jack. And he was one of the most charismatic men she had ever known.

"Grrrrh!" she muttered, finally making the package presentable enough to take back to him.

"That looks great."

"It's okay. Nancy, my helper, is the one who usually does the wrapping."

"Well, I'm satisfied."

She didn't respond. There wasn't anything left to say. She just wished he'd go. Unfortunately, he showed no sign of doing that.

"There was a third reason I stopped by."

Again Katherine's eyebrows arched. So Lee Ann had shot off her mouth after all. "Look—"

"Will you have dinner with me Saturday?"

She blinked. "Did you say dinner?"

"I thought so." He laughed. "I sure hope I haven't started stuttering."

Her mouth turned down. "Funny."

"Shall I pick you up, say, around sevenish?"

"I don't think that's a good idea, our having dinner, that is."

"Why not?"

She opened her mouth only to snap it shut again. There were a multitude of reasons, but none she cared to share with him, at least not now, not when she saw a long-standing customer and a gossiper to boot pull up in front of the shop. Hence, she had to get rid of him. Now.

"All right," she said, not bothering to hide her agitation. "Seven it is."

He grinned, then turned when the front-door buzzer went off. When he swung back around, he winked. "I'll see you."

"Wow, who was that?" Patsy Middlebrook demanded, her eyes following Bryce out the door.

"You don't want to know," Katherine snapped.

Patsy gave her an incredulous look. "Yes, I do."

Katherine sighed. "He's Bryce Burnette, pastor of the United Nondenominational Church."

"He's a minister? Holy Moses. I've never had one who looked like him."

"Neither have I."

"So?"

"So," Katherine countered tersely.

"So I saw the way he looked at you."

"You didn't see anything of the sort," Katherine said with heat.

Patsy laughed. "Boy, did I blow your skirt tail up."

"This conversation is over." Katherine glared at her.

"Whatever you say."

"How 'bout some tea?" Katherine asked, changing the subject.

"Sounds good. While you're getting it, I'm going to go through your new party dresses."

"Help yourself."

Once Katherine was in the back room preparing the coffee, she paused and tried to gather her scattered wits. What had she done? Something stupid. She couldn't in her wildest dreams imagine herself going out with a minister or anyone else beholden to the public for that matter.

Suddenly she leaned against the counter, feeling completely drained.

"One hundred and twenty for, and fifty against."

Clapping and shouts of amen followed the announcement of the vote.

"Congratulations, Pastor."

"Thanks, Wilbur," Bryce said to another in a long line of many well-wishers. "I appreciate all your efforts on seeing this vote through to the end."

"It's the Lord, Bryce. He wants us to have a new facility."

"I couldn't agree more."

That conversation had taken place over an hour ago now, and Bryce was at home in the parsonage, standing at the window, staring out at the star-riddled sky.

What a great victory, he thought, thinking back on the vote that had been cast earlier that evening in a specially called service. Now he was alone, weary yet pumped up, so pumped in fact that sleep was the furthest thing from his mind.

But the bed of roses wouldn't be without its thorns, he reminded himself. The detractors wouldn't keep their mutterings to themselves. He was sure of that. And there would be other potholes as well, such as raising the sum of money needed to eventually pay off what they had to borrow. But he wouldn't think about the cons. He would deal with them when the time came.

Right now he was rejoicing in a great victory, actually two victories, he corrected himself mentally. By golly, he was having dinner with Katherine Mays.

Amazing? Yes. Smart? No.

When he'd walked into her shop and seen her again, and seen the type of garments she sold, he'd told himself to turn around and head straight back out the door.

He hadn't.

Instead he'd stared into that lovely face and *only* his good intentions had gone out the door. A strangled sound left his throat as he rubbed the back of his neck.

What was there about the woman that made him hunger for sexual contact? He had almost given up on ever feeling that "spark" again, especially with someone who was so different from his wife.

But there was something unique about Katherine Mays, something intriguing and titillating, and he was captivated. Yet underneath that sassy outer wrapping, he sensed a depth of vulnerability which made the prize that much more tempting.

He let out a slow, pent-up breath as his gaze swung around to the phone. ''Call her and cancel,'' he muttered. ''It's not too late.''

The phone didn't move, but then neither did he.

Seven

She had taken leave of her senses, no doubt about it. So what was she going to do about that? The right thing, Katherine's conscience answered. *The smart thing*. She would call him and tell him she couldn't go to dinner, that something had come up. She'd invent that "something," if that was what it took to jolt herself back on track.

Letting out a slow breath, she took a sip of hot green tea and waited for the soothing effect to calm her. But it didn't do the trick. Her insides were still scrambled along with her brain.

Katherine took another sip, then peered at the clock on the bedside table. Seven o'clock. Groaning, she put her cup down, then flopped back onto her pillow.

So much for sleeping in, one of the rare Saturdays that she treated herself, letting Nancy open up and work alone for a few hours. Traditionally Saturdays were slow, or at least the morning hours.

She squeezed her eyes shut. That didn't work, either. She might as well get up and go run a couple of miles. Maybe that would get her over the heebie-jeebies.

When she returned, she would call the Reverend Bryce Burnette and break their date for that evening. Now that he'd thought about it, he probably regretted asking her out, anyway. That made her feel better, but only for a few moments. If he hadn't wanted to go out with her, he would've called her earlier, not at the last minute.

"Damn!"

Okay, so she wasn't blessed with all of his fine attributes. So she was a loathsome worm for going back on her word at the last minute. She could live with that. Besides, she'd be doing him a favor. There was no point in their even having a friendly dinner. It would be a waste of her time and his.

A party girl fraternizing with a preacher. What a hoot, she thought, giggling aloud, a giggle that bordered on hysteria. But that giggle soon died a natural death, and Katherine sobered, cursing the luck of the draw that he wasn't an accountant, or something as equally prosaic.

She kicked back the cover, sat on the side of the bed, then peered out the window. Was that rain she heard? On closer observation, she saw that it was.

Well, she wasn't about to get out and run in rainy weather and get sick.

Instead, she would build a fire in the living room and curl up with some more tea and a good book. Yeah, right. After she called Bryce, that is, she reminded herself, his smiling face suddenly leaping to the forefront of her mind.

Another groan escaped her as her stomach tightened. No, she wouldn't weaken. She *would* call him. Okay, she was weakening. Perhaps she did want to see him—all the more reason why she shouldn't.

The indisputable fact was she'd already been involved with a man in the public eye whose job put certain constraints on her lifestyle, leaving her stifled and feeling as though she lived in a fishbowl. She couldn't handle that or her politico husband, and she could see the same problems looming here.

More than that, what she had gone through with Jack because of that lifestyle had left her in an emotional ditch, wrecked and mangled.

No man was worth that. Her heart was sealed shut, and it would remain that way. Love 'em and leave 'em was the motto she lived by.

Good grief, she chided herself severely. The man hadn't asked her to marry him or make a lifetime commitment. He had just asked her out to dinner. What harm could possibly come from that?

None.

Then, why couldn't she give herself a break, stop beating up on herself and behave like the grown-up that she was? No reason. Wilting with relief, Katherine stood and was about to head back to the kitchen and the teapot when the phone rang.

It was Lee Ann.

"I didn't wake you up, did I?"

"No, but I wish you had."

"Uh-oh, what's wrong?"

Lee Ann knew her too well. And right now, Katherine didn't want her friend to know about her having dinner with Bryce. Lord, talk about stirring up a hornet's nest. She shuddered to think what Lee Ann's reaction would be.

"Hey, you still there?"

"Sorry," Katherine muttered lamely, "I don't have it together yet."

"What time are you going into the shop?"

"Around noon."

"Great."

"What does that mean?" Katherine asked in a leery tone.

"It means we can meet for breakfast and get started talking about the decorating plans for the church. Praise the Lord, the vote passed, so we're in business."

"Oh, Lee Ann, I—"

"Oh, come on. It'll do you good. Anyway, you promised you'd help, so don't think you're going to wimp out now, because you're not."

"I guess that told me," Katherine said flatly, though her tone was laced with guarded humor.

"I was toying with calling Bryce and asking him to meet us. What do you think?"

Katherine panicked. "Uh, I don't think that's such a good idea."

"Why not?"

She had to do some fast verbal dancing. "We're not ready for his input yet."

"I guess you're right. It's just that I'm so excited, I can't wait to get started."

"Me, too," Katherine said drolly.

Lee Ann laughed, then said in a droll tone of her own, "I can tell."

"Look, I'll meet you at our favorite dive in, say, an hour."

Whew, she'd managed to dodge that bullet, she told herself, finally getting up and heading to the bathroom.

The thought of having breakfast *and* dinner with Bryce was more than unsettling, it was actually more than she could handle.

Katherine stared at herself in the mirror. Would she pass muster? Absolutely. Without exception. She had chosen a simple black dress, not too short and not too tight. Yet it seemed to nip and tuck in just the right places, which gave her normally slender figure a more voluptuous look.

Especially her breasts.

Would Bryce notice? Suddenly her cheeks flamed, and she sucked in her breath. Where on earth had that thought come from? She didn't know and didn't want to. With fingers that weren't quite steady, she put on her earrings, muttering curse words under her breath.

And she was about to have dinner with a preacher. Shame on her.

The doorbell chimed.

Katherine frowned and stared at the clock. Bryce was nearly an hour early, which she guessed was all right considering she was dressed. Still, her frown deepened. What if she hadn't been ready? She figured he'd be punctual—it fit his personality. But an hour— that was a bit of a stretch.

Oh, well, it was no big deal. Anyhow, the sooner they had dinner, the sooner she would get back home, back to her safety net. Under the circumstances, there was a lot to say for that.

"Coming," Katherine called out, scurrying to the door.

When she yanked it open, her mouth gaped. It wasn't Bryce who stood in front of her but Nancy. Katherine's eyes widened, and she cried, "Oh, my God."

"Can…I come in?" Nancy stammered.

Without answering her, Katherine took her gently by the arm and led her to the sofa, all the while fighting back her own tears. "What happened?" she asked, easing down beside Nancy.

Nancy opened her mouth, but no words were forthcoming, which didn't surprise Katherine. Her coworker looked as if she'd been in a street brawl and had definitely come out the loser.

Her face was battered and bruised, her lips were split and swollen, and she moved as if her bones had been disjointed. Most likely they had, Katherine thought in horror.

"You should be in the hospital."

"No, please!" Nancy cried, clutching at Katherine's arm while visibly withering in pain.

Katherine pushed Nancy's damp hair off her forehead. "What happened? Who did this to you?"

Nancy's head dropped, and her shoulders shook. "Wally."

"Wally," Katherine repeated, dumbfounded.

Granted, she had never liked Nancy's husband, had always thought he was lazy and no good, but she had never in a million years guessed him to be an abuser. No matter, the proof was before her.

Her panic burgeoned. "Where are the boys?"

"With a friend."

"Are they okay?"

Nancy lifted her tear-ravaged face. "He didn't touch them."

"Thank God for small favors."

"Oh, Katherine," she sobbed, "I don't know what to do."

"Right now, I'm going to doctor your face and get you some tea." She paused. "I'd feel a lot better, though, if you'd let me take you to the emergency room. What if you have some broken bones?"

"I promise I don't. He just shoved me around."

"In between slugging you." Katherine's eyes sparked. "Damn him to hell."

It wouldn't do for her to get her hands on that bastard. She'd like nothing better than to take a club and work him over. Let him see how it felt. Instead, she'd have to be content to let the police work him over within the law. Somehow, though, that didn't seem fair.

"I'll be right back."

Later, after making Nancy as comfortable as possible, Katherine remained beside her and held her hand. "You know you're going to have to file charges."

Nancy's closed eyes shot open, filling with terror. "He warned me not to do that."

"You have to do it, anyway. You have no choice. This isn't the first time he's hit you, right?"

"Actually, it is," Nancy said in an honest voice, "though he's threatened plenty of times."

"Was he drunk?"

"Yes."

"Well, that doesn't excuse him. Actually, that makes it worse."

Nancy heaved a sigh. "I know."

"So, again, you have to turn him in."

"I don't think I can."

"Why not? Next time you might not be so lucky and get away from him. You have to think of the boys."

"I'm aware of all that. But I'm afraid of him."

"And well you should be, which is all the more reason to file charges."

"You couldn't possibly understand," Nancy wailed, her voice tormented.

"That's where you're wrong."

Nancy stared at her through swollen eyes. "You mean—"

"I don't mean anything," Katherine said hastily. "This is not about me. It's about you and the boys."

Nancy shook her head. "When he's not drinking, he's good to us."

Katherine swallowed her retort and her frustration. She couldn't make Nancy do what was right. She could only advise, which probably was the smartest move on her part. Nancy needed professional help; a minister would do for starters.

Oh, Lord! She had forgotten about Bryce, who was due anytime now.

"What's wrong?" Nancy asked as if sensing something was wrong.

"Uh, nothing." Katherine stood. "Nothing important, that is. I was going out to dinner."

"Oh, I'm sorry. I'll go."

"You'll do no such thing."

"But I can't bear the thought of anyone else seeing me like this."

"That's not a problem. You just stay put while I make a phone call."

Once she'd looked up Bryce's number, she punched it out and waited, her fingers crossed.

Eight

"Is anything wrong?"

"No," Katherine said.

That didn't jibe, Bryce thought, and he almost said as much. If nothing was amiss, then he would be at her house about now or close to it.

"Look, I'm...sorry to cancel at the last minute."

He picked up on the hint of anxiety in her voice and knew she was groping for a suitable explanation or at least one that he would buy. However, he wasn't buying, not at the moment, anyway.

He squelched his irritation. True, he had questioned his sanity in asking her to dinner, yet he wasn't at all happy that she'd broken the date just as he was about to walk out the door.

"Look, I know what you must be thinking," Katherine said into the uncomfortable and growing silence, "but I have a really good reason for my actions."

"I'm sure you do."

Desperation. Was that the edge he heard in her voice now? Or was he trying to give her more credit than she deserved?

"Is there anything I can do?"

"No, thanks," she said briskly. Then as if she realized she'd been short, she went on to say, "But I appreciate your offering."

"Anytime." He tried to hold his temper and his sarcasm at bay, but he didn't think he'd done a very good job.

He was disappointed. That was the bottom line. Even though he knew she had probably done him a big favor by ducking out, he realized now that deep down he wanted to be with her, that, rational or irrational, he was completely smitten.

He flinched at the confession, wondering what his mother, as well as his congregation, would think about that. His lips turned into a smirk. Was there ever a time when he wasn't conscious of his image and what other people thought?

"You're not upset, are you?"

Again her voice, slightly raspy now, jerked him back to the moment at hand. "Yes, as a matter of fact, I am."

"Well, again, I'm sorry."

"I am, too. Would you mind if I called you later?"

A long hesitation. "No."

"Later, then."

He was about to hang up when he heard her say, "Bryce."

His hopes burgeoned along with his heart. "Yes."

"Uh, nothing. I...have to go."

The dial tone suddenly assaulted his ear. After staring at the receiver for a long moment, he replaced it gently. What he'd wanted to do was slam it down.

He whipped around to toss his jacket on the sofa and caught a glimpse of himself in the mirror that hung above an antique library table.

He grimaced, noticing that his lips were drawn in a thin line and that the hand he shoved through his hair was not quite steady. Great. Just great.

A date. That was all it was. She just broke a date. He was a big boy; he could accept that. No, he couldn't, because he didn't want to. Again, he wanted to be with her, have her zap him with that high-wattage smile of hers, hear her laughter, see that twinkle in her eyes.

His gut was on fire, and he couldn't seem to put it out, for more than one reason. Sure, his base instincts were stirred; he wouldn't deny that. Yet he remained convinced something was wrong, that something had happened.

What if she really needed help and had been too proud or uncomfortable asking him? Even though he was a pastor, he wasn't *her* pastor which made a big difference. So he should just leave it be, chalk it up to a bummer evening and forget it. Forget *her*.

He paced back and forth across the living room floor, the fire in his gut spreading with every step.

"This is baloney," he finally muttered, then grabbed his coat and headed out the door, slamming it behind him.

Nancy's eyes widened and she cringed.

"Hey, don't worry." Katherine's eyes darkened as she made her way to the door, having heard the bell chime. "It's going to be okay. I'm not going to let anything else happen to you."

"What if it's Wally?"

Katherine stopped in her tracks and swung around. "No way. He wouldn't dare come here. He knows better."

Nancy's breath was audible. "You're right. He wouldn't have the nerve."

"Whoever it is, I'll get rid of them."

"Look, why don't I go?" Nancy was growing more agitated by the second.

"Forget that," Katherine said emphatically.

"I can go to my mother's. I've already forced you into changing your plans. I feel so bad—"

"I said forget it. My plans were not important. But yours are. What you do right now, the decision you make, will affect the rest of your life." She gave Nancy a reassuring smile. "I'm not expecting anyone else, so whoever it is won't get inside the door."

She shouldn't have been shocked when she jerked open the door and Bryce was standing there. But she was. And livid. How dare he encroach on her privacy this way?

Ah, but he was a minister and, like politicians, they thought no one could do without them. Realizing she was probably being harder on Bryce than he deserved, she felt a moment of contrition. But it didn't last long. He shouldn't have come.

"My instincts told me you were in trouble," Bryce said without mincing words.

Katherine struggled to get her bearings as he suddenly looked so calm and solid standing there that she wanted to grab him and hold on to him.

"Well, your instincts were wrong," she said in a low, terse tone.

He shrugged, but his eyes kept their piercing glint. "This wasn't a good idea, was it?"

Katherine gripped the doorknob tighter. "No, it wasn't."

"Again, are you sure you're all right?"

"Yes. So please go." She had lowered her voice to a whisper, which she knew added to his concern and curiosity. But if she didn't remain in control of the situation, Nancy would bolt, especially at the sight of a man, any man.

To his credit, Bryce didn't cast any furtive glances beyond her shoulder to see what was going on, if anything. Yet she knew he couldn't help but notice that she was dressed to go out. She shuddered to think what was going through his mind, especially when he was staring at her as though he were probing her soul.

She flushed, then looked away.

"I'll call you soon, okay?"

Katherine cast her gaze back to him and nodded, biting down on her lower lip.

He turned and made his way down the sidewalk. When he got to his car, he turned again, giving her a heartfelt and reassuring smile. Her knees almost buckled under her. They would have if she hadn't been clinging to the doorknob.

Suddenly she really didn't want him to go. Nancy was a huge responsibility that loomed larger by the moment. Too, what had happened to Nancy had stirred her own dark memories.

But her co-worker needed her, and she couldn't let her down. She would just have to push aside her own troubled thoughts and deal with what was before her. She was capable, probably as capable as any minister, including Bryce.

The disastrous visit to her pastor that one time jumped back to mind. She winced. Somehow she didn't think Bryce would be that type of counselor, but she didn't know.

Hell, she didn't know anything about him other than who he was and how good he looked. *And how much she wanted him.*

Did she really want to have sex with a preacher?

As if something was chasing her, she slammed the door shut on both Bryce and her thoughts.

"You look like you've had a good time. Did you tie one on last night with one of your dancing rednecks?"

"No, I did not."

Lee Ann's eyebrows shot up. "Hey, you don't have to snap my head off."

"Sorry, I didn't mean to."

"Is something going on I ought to know about?"

"Probably."

"Then tell me."

They were in Lee Ann's interior design shop on a Monday afternoon with fabric, wall coverings, etcetera strewn over a large table, trying to decide on colors for the sanctuary as well as the church offices.

"By the way, where are the other committee members?" Katherine asked.

Lee Ann's face lost a tinge of its color and for a second she averted her gaze, which instantly raised a red flag. "You wouldn't," Katherine said flatly.

"Yeah, I would," Lee Ann admitted, throwing Katherine a cautious look. "Actually, I did."

"You mean it's just us, that you haven't appointed anyone else?"

"Not so far," Lee Ann admitted reluctantly. "And that's the way I'd like to keep it." Her tone now held a note of belligerence.

Katherine was flabbergasted. "Why, that's crazy. This is an awesome job, and I can't spend that kind of time on it and neither can you. Right?"

"No, but there's no one else I want to work with at the church," Lee Ann wailed.

"Keep looking. You'll find someone."

Lee Ann gave her a look. "All right, I'll try."

Katherine eyed her with skepticism.

"Bryce'll be thrilled when he learns you're on board the project," Lee Ann said, changing the subject.

Katherine's heart skipped a beat. "So you haven't told him?"

"Not yet, but I will."

"He might not want me helping you." Katherine forced her voice to remain emotionless.

"Are you kidding? He'll think I've pulled off a coup, though I'll admit he might be a bit taken aback."

"I think that's an understatement," Katherine said with sarcasm. "I'm beginning to think I've lost my mind."

"Oh, pooh," Lee Ann said. "Where's your sense of adventure? It'll be fun, especially when it turns out to be absolutely gorgeous."

"I hope you're right."

"Now back to what made you look so drawn and tired."

Knowing that she could trust Lee Ann, Katherine gave her a thumbnail sketch of Nancy's situation.

"Oh, how horrible," Lee Ann responded. "And the fact that she dragged you into it is also horrible."

"Well, at least she agreed to go seek help from the Women's Shelter, which is a start."

"I'm assuming she's still working, or you wouldn't be here."

"Actually, she isn't. She's too battered and bruised. I have someone else, Becky Jo Beard, who's pitching in. She's a really good customer, plus she has some retail sales experience."

"Great."

"Now you know why you can't depend on me as much as you'd like."

"I hear you. But promise you'll stay out of that situation with Nancy and her lame husband. It can't be good for you."

Katherine ignored that last pointed remark. "I'm okay. I'd just like to get a shot at the jerk myself."

"All the more reason to keep your distance." Lee Ann paused. "Have you thought about talking to Bryce? Or better yet, encouraging Nancy to talk to him? He's great with that sort of thing. The best, actually."

Katherine hoped her friend wouldn't notice how her heart upped its beat. Just mentioning his name had that effect on her.

"No. I haven't had the courage yet, though I'm not sure that's the best way for her to go. At the moment men in general tend to freak her out."

They were silent for a while, then Lee Ann begin tidying up the table. "It's past time to call it a day. You're bushed and so am I." She leaned over and gave Katherine a brief hug. "Thanks for coming. Go home and soak your tired bones in the tub and have a glass of wine."

"Good idea. In fact that sounds wonderful."

Lee Ann grinned impishly. "I can think of something even better."

"Oh?"

"A bottle of wine and a man in the bath with you."

Again Bryce came to Katherine's mind, bringing a tell-tale flush to her face. "You're full of it," she mumbled as she grabbed her purse and hurried out the door.

Five minutes later Katherine was turning into her own drive when a car pulled up to the curb. Her stomach took a nosedive.

It was Bryce.

Nine

What was *he* doing here?

Her heart was pounding so hard she couldn't get the key out of the ignition. Hells bells! She had to do something to calm herself. She was behaving like some sex-starved junkie. Why he continued to arouse such unexpected and unwanted excitement in her was beyond all reasoning.

The answer was to get rid of him once and for all. And while she was at it, she would tell Lee Ann she'd have to get someone else to help with the renovations. For her own peace of mind, if nothing else, she had to stay away from Pastor Burnette.

By the time Katherine scrambled out of the car, he was there, stopping within touching distance of her.

For a long, awkward moment, no words were exchanged.

Their eyes simply met and held. Blue eyes delved into brown ones. Katherine wanted to turn away, but she couldn't. She seemed to be lost in those incredible eyes of his and vice versa.

Finally Bryce broke the silence and not a minute too soon. She realized that during that silence she hadn't taken a decent breath.

"Hi."

She giggled suddenly, which proved to be the release valve they both needed. He followed suit with a deep chuckle.

"Aren't you going to respond?" he asked, a teasing glint now in those eyes.

"I thought I did," she said inanely.

He threw his head back and laughed. Katherine's legs turned to liquid, and if she hadn't been close enough to lean against her vehicle, she might have lost her balance.

That was all the more reason for her to smarten up and send him on his way without even hearing why he'd come in the first place.

But the fact that he was a man of God and the fact that poor manners were not her modus operandi, she decided to cool it.

"Are you still mad at me?"

She blinked, that question shocking her. "Mad?"

"Yeah, when I appeared at your door unexpectedly."

"Oh, that." Katherine shifted uncomfortably. He

was right. She should've still been peeved at him for that stunt. But when he'd parked that gorgeous body in front of her just now, all other thoughts fled. His presence filled her mind to full capacity.

"Yeah, that." He was still smiling.

"I know I should be," she responded with caution, "but since I know you meant no harm, then I guess all is forgiven."

"You guess?"

"Okay, you're forgiven," she said sheepishly. No way could she or anyone else stay mad at someone who looked like him.

"Good, then how 'bout going for coffee?"

Katherine blinked again. "Now?"

"Yes, now."

Seconds ticked by.

"Do you have other plans?" he asked.

"No, but—"

"But what?"

She shrugged, then flashed him a smile tinged with defeat. "Nothing. It looks like you've caught me flat-footed."

He chuckled again. "Then let's go."

Fifteen minutes later they were seated in the corner of a small restaurant with two cups of cafe latte in front of them. Another highly charged silence filled the air as she met his sensual gaze.

Uncomfortable with the situation, Katherine shifted in the seat and looked away.

"You don't like me much, do you?"

Katherine swung around, her eyes huge. "What?"

"You heard me," he said in a drawling tone.

He was leaning forward now, his gaze pinning her, clear and steady. Her face felt hot and she wanted to squirm, but she didn't. She didn't back down, either.

"I don't know you well enough to make that judgment."

He took a sip of his coffee, though he continued to look at her above the rim. "Oh, I think you do."

She sipped from her coffee, even though it burned her throat.

"Or is it the fact that I'm a minister that makes you uptight?"

She bristled. "I'm not uptight."

"Sorry." He gave her a sheepish smile which relieved some of the growing tension. "Maybe that wasn't the right choice of words."

"You're right, though. I'm not comfortable around clergy."

"Is there a particular reason for that?"

"Yes." Her tone was clipped in spite of her efforts to the contrary.

"Someone hurt you?"

She sighed. "Yes, he did."

"Katherine." His eyes and voice pulled her back toward him. "Just remember I would never do that."

Oh, Lord, when he looked at her like that, her entire system went haywire.

"I'd rather not talk about it."

"Maybe some other time, then?"

"Maybe."

He let out a breath, then changed the subject. "So how's your friend?"

"Lee Ann?"

"No." He smiled, only to have it suddenly disappear.

For a second she was disappointed, feeling as if a cloud had covered the sun.

"I mean the one who was at your house."

Katherine stiffened, and when she spoke her tone was cold. "Is that what this invitation's all about?"

"No, I wanted to see you," he said in a husky voice.

That voice. It oozed sex the same as his eyes and his lips. She felt her insides start a meltdown.

"Then don't pry," she said in a shaky voice.

"I don't mean to pry. I mean to help."

Katherine gave him a thin smile.

"Look, no way could I miss seeing the woman on your sofa, black eye and all."

Irritated with his persistence, she said, "So you did. But I'd rather not discuss it. It's not my call to do so."

His eyes darkened. "Well, again, if you need me, I'm available."

That's what I'm afraid of.

Thrusting that unsettling thought aside, Katherine nodded, then concentrated on her coffee, wondering again what on earth possessed her to waste her time coming here with him. Any kind of personal relationship between them was impossible. They were from two different planets, for Pete's sake.

Then why did she feel the sudden urge to confide in him again like she had the other evening, concerning herself and Nancy? But she couldn't. The words were locked in her throat, and she would choke on them before she could let them go.

"My mom loved her pin."

"I thought she would."

Grateful to be back on safe ground, Katherine gave him a brilliant smile and watched as he sucked in his breath. Or maybe that was wishful thinking on her part.

"Do you always say what's on your mind?" he finally asked, his lips twitching.

"Most of the time, I have to admit."

"Mom was a bit surprised, though, when she saw where it came from." He was smiling now.

"Oh, really?"

"Yep."

"Why was that?" she asked innocently, her tongue wandering across her lower lip.

For a second he didn't answer, seemingly fascinated by the sight. He cleared his throat and said, "She's a bit old for party dresses and lingerie, and that's what you sell, after all."

In spite of herself, Katherine's face turned red. Hearing him say the word *lingerie* seemed to put their conversation on a different level again, a more personal one.

As if he sensed that, too, their eyes reconnected. She turned away from the heat that shone from his.

"If you're in church Sunday," he said in a normal tone, "she'll have it on."

He was hinting, she knew. And while she had no intention of returning to church, she was reluctant to admit that. At the moment things were on an even keel, and she didn't want to upset the applecart.

"I'm betting it'll look smashing, too."

He smiled. "You bet it will. My mother's still a handsome woman."

"I'd like to meet her sometime."

"That can be arranged."

Oh, brother, she'd put her foot in her mouth again. Would she ever learn?

"So when you're not working, what do you like to do for fun?"

A reprieve. Safe ground again. "Travel and dance."

He gave her an incredulous look.

She shrugged. "You asked."

"That I did," he said, another smile rearranging those sexy lips. "So you're a party girl."

"And you're a minister."

His face sobered. "So what are you saying?"

"You figure it out."

"I already have, but it doesn't matter."

"You must know I'm divorced."

"I do." His eyes were probing. "And I'm a widower."

"Which spells trouble," she said bluntly.

He tossed back his head and laughed. "I can handle trouble. How 'bout you?"

"I—"

Suddenly the waitress appeared at their table, leaving the check. Katherine could've jumped up and hugged her, the conversation having gotten way out of hand again.

Once she shuffled off, Bryce peered at his watch, then back up at her. "I suppose you need to go."

"Yes, I do. I have a long, hard week in front of me."

He rose and soon they were in his car. The drive to her house was done in virtual silence and not a comfortable one either. From time to time Katherine felt his gaze rest on her. She knew he found her different and perhaps exciting, as she did him.

But to take that feeling any further would be crazy.

He shoved the car in park in her drive but didn't make any effort to open the door. Instead he opened the windows, then clicked off the ignition.

The air that filtered through the windows was cool and sweet smelling. She inhaled and listened to crickets sing their nightly lullaby. It was late, and she should go inside. She kept telling herself that, yet she didn't move. If was as if he and the night had her mesmerized.

"Katherine."

The husky sound of her name drew her around to him. His face was close, too close. And for a second she fought for a decent breath.

"I want to see you again," he whispered. He didn't touch her, but he might as well have. His words and voice were a caress in themselves.

She swallowed against the heat that rose up the back of her throat. "I don't think that's a good idea."

"Why?"

"I can name several reasons."

"Whatever they are, they're not important."

She laughed a shaky laugh. "Things are not that simple."

"They are if you make them."

"Are you always this hardheaded?"

He smiled, then it faded. "Only when I want something—in this case someone—very badly." His face moved closer.

Dear God, he was going to kiss her, and every nerve in her body screamed for him to do just that.

"Katherine," he said again, "I—"

The cellular phone in his right pocket suddenly rang.

He froze, then let out a savage groan. Her stomach churned as she listened to the one-sided conversation with her eyes closed and her arms across her trembling body.

"I have to go," he said in a low and not so steady tone.

"Then go."

His eyebrows rose. "One of my members has been in a car accident."

"Oh, dear, I'm sorry."

He gave her a pained look. "No, I'm sorry."

"Don't be," she said dully. "You're just doing your job, right?"

"I'll call you."

"Don't bother," she said in sharp tone.

"Hey, that's not—"

"Save it. I have to go and so do you."

She scrambled out of the car and practically ran to the door without so much as a backward glance.

Only after she was inside and leaning against the door did she hear him drive away.

Ten

"**I** think it has possibilities."

After parking her car in front of the boutique, Paula Lamber turned and gave Katherine a quizzical look. "So are you really interested in leasing it?"

"Yes, but I'm still not convinced I can swing operating two stores, not yet, anyway."

"I just hate to see you give that place up. It seems ideal for what you're looking for."

It was ideal. And Katherine appreciated the Realtor calling her that morning a few minutes after she'd arrived at the store, telling her about a small building on the other side of town that had just lost its tenant. Since it hadn't been time to open, she'd opted for a quick look-see.

"How long can you give me to make up my mind?" Katherine asked.

Paula chewed on the inside of her mouth, a habit that would drive Katherine up the wall if she were around her very much. "Several days, but no more. That strip mall's hot right now."

"But you do have the exclusive on that particular location, right?"

"Right."

Katherine opened the door, then smiled. "I'll let you know. And thanks again."

What to do? Katherine asked herself for the umpteenth time as she unlocked the door. Suddenly her life had taken several unexpected turns, leaving her feeling confused and overwhelmed.

"Hey."

Katherine pulled up short at the sound of the unexpected voice. Nancy was back. Praise the Lord. While Becky Jo had been fine, she wasn't Nancy, which meant that Katherine herself had had to spend a lot of time manning the front. Hence, the paperwork had piled up on her desk which was another thing that added to her frustration.

Nancy came out of the office with a smile on her face, but her eyes weren't smiling. Katherine wrestled with mixed feelings of sympathy and disappointment. Nancy was there, but so were her troubles.

Wordlessly Katherine gave her a hug. When they parted, tears filled Nancy's eyes.

"Sorry, but I can't seem to stop crying."

"No apologies necessary. I'm just glad to see

you.'' Katherine paused and scrutinized her closely. ''All the tell-all signs have gone.''

''Otherwise I wouldn't have been here.''

''Well, you're here and that's what counts.''

Nancy motioned toward the back. ''I made some coffee.''

''I'm ready.'' Katherine headed that way, flinching as a clap of thunder rocked the building. ''I just did make it back, didn't I?''

Nancy didn't answer until they both had coffee and were sitting at the café table. ''I was hoping it wouldn't rain today. It makes me bluer.''

''I can understand that. So how's it going at the shelter?''

''I left there yesterday and moved in with Mother.''

Katherine frowned. ''Do you think that's wise? I mean, Wally seems to have a way of getting around your mother.''

Nancy's features hardened. ''Not this time, especially after I filed charges.''

''Which was a smart thing to do.''

''If it hadn't been for you and the people at the shelter, I would never have had the courage.''

''So what now?''

''I don't know,'' Nancy said, her eyes filling with a new batch of tears. ''The kids are the only thing that keeps me from doing something stupid.''

''Oh, Nancy,'' Katherine said in an anxious tone. ''Don't even talk like that, much less think it.''

''I just don't know what to do,'' Nancy wailed. ''I

feel like this is all my fault, that I did something wrong.''

''Stop it! You did nothing except love him, and he took advantage of that.''

Nancy's hands trembled as she reached for her cup. ''For now, he's leaving us alone.''

''Filing charges makes abuse a whole new ball game.''

''Only time will tell,'' Nancy said forlornly.

Katherine had to squelch the urge to shake her employee. Couldn't she see she was wasting her time and her life on that no-good scumbag?

''I know you've had counseling at the shelter, but there's someone else I want you to talk to.''

Nancy gave her a suspicious look. ''Who?''

''Bryce Burnette.''

''Who's that?''

''A minister.''

''Oh, I don't think—''

''Please. For me.''

''What makes you think he can help me?''

Katherine wished she knew the answer to that, but she didn't. Maybe it was what Lee Ann had told her about him or what she had gleaned from talking with him herself. She didn't know, but something told her that Bryce with his gentle strength could help her friend put her life back on track.

Katherine shuddered inwardly. The fact that he had sent *her* life careening off course was another matter altogether, one that she couldn't afford to think about, not now, anyway.

"All right," Nancy finally said, though without joy. "That's the least I can do for you."

"Don't do it for me. It's important that you see him for yourself and not anyone else, except maybe your boys."

"I'll see him," Nancy said, then reached for a tissue and wiped her eyes.

"I'll set the meeting up and let you know." Katherine blew out a long breath. "Now have we ever got work to do."

"Who was that who just dropped you off?"

Katherine explained.

"So what are you going to do?"

"I'm not sure. At this point I think I have more on my plate with this store than I can handle. Too, I simply don't have the liquid cash that I need right now."

Nancy squeezed Katherine's hand. "It'll work out. If you lose that site, there'll be another one when the time's right."

"Thanks," Katherine said, giving her a lame smile. "So what's first on the day's agenda?"

Katherine grimaced. "The lingerie trunk show. Do you realize it's only three days away?"

"No, but since the invitations have gone out," Nancy replied, "we'll be in great shape. So stop worrying."

Every bone in her body ached and not from the running track, either. As Nancy promised, everything had come together for tomorrow's big show. The flowers and favors were in place. And first thing in the morning the catering company would come with the food.

With Christmas in mind, she had high hopes for big sales. Meanwhile she also had hopes of getting a good night's sleep. She had fixed herself a bite to eat and taken a bath. All she had to do now was crawl between the sheets and close her eyes.

Katherine's gaze sought the clock in the living room. Eight. Heavens, that was too early to hit the sack. Maybe if she read awhile, she could unwind. However, when she curled her legs under her on the sofa and opened her novel, Bryce's face blurred the words on the page.

Slamming the book shut, she rested her head against the cushion and struggled to get air through her lungs. What was there about him that kept her body on full alert? When he was around, she was conscious of herself in a way she'd never experienced before.

She should never have been cajoled into going on that coffee jaunt. It had turned their acquaintance into something really personal. He had come close to kissing her. No doubt about it. His breath fanning her face and that look in his eyes had said as much.

Bedroom eyes.

Her cheeks flamed. God bless America! She was talking about a preacher. But preachers did it, too, she reminded herself fiercely, while fighting off a funny feeling that invaded her stomach at the thought of what he'd be like in bed.

When his cell phone had rung, she had wanted to scream. Then cold reality had set in, and that feeling of heady excitement disappeared along with the ache deep inside her.

He was at the mercy of others. His time belonged to the people he served, not to himself. That was a fact that would never change. A preacher and a politician, so different, so alike.

She'd already been down that street filled with huge potholes and had no intention of traveling it again. When she'd told Bryce not to bother to call her, she'd meant it.

That was why she'd tried *not* to think about him. Until now she'd been successful, having made up her mind that Bryce was *not* for her.

So why couldn't she erase thoughts of him from her mind?

Another serious relationship was not in the cards, and she suspected everything Bryce did was serious. And marriage—ha, that was most definitely out. A husband, 2.3 children and a brick house in suburbia was not for her.

Yet somehow Bryce with his vulnerable sexiness had managed to invade the nooks and crannies of her mind and stay there as if he had the right. Well, he damn sure didn't.

Suddenly the phone rang. Grateful for the respite from her thoughts, she reached for it.

"Thanks for the invite."

Bryce.

When she heard that voice, her stomach always did

funny things, and despite the lecture to herself, this evening was no exception. She clutched the receiver while she forced her tongue off the roof of her mouth so that she could speak.

"Do you think I should come?" he asked into the silence, his voice filled with suppressed humor.

"I don't know what you're talking about," she said with sincerity, though there was a breathlessness in her voice that she despised.

He chuckled outright. "To your lingerie show."

"You mean—"

His chuckle deepened. "Yep. I'm holding the invitation in my hand even as we speak."

"Oh, dear."

She was mortified but not surprised, now that she thought about it. When he had bought the pin for his mother, his name had automatically been entered into the cash register which was in itself a computer. The invitation list had come from that.

"Katherine."

"What can I say?" Suddenly the humor in it all hit her and she laughed. "It's a done deal."

"Trust me, I'm not offended. Actually, I'm intrigued with the idea."

"Surely you're not coming?"

"Would it upset you if I did?"

"Yes."

He laughed. "At least you're honest."

A short silence fell over the phone line, but even at that, Katherine was aware of the crackling tension.

"Have you given any more thought to what I said the other night?" he asked, changing the subject.

"About what?" she asked innocently, her heart rate elevating.

"My seeing you again."

His voice had lowered several decibels, making him sound sexier than ever. Damn him, didn't he get it? "I've already told you that's not a good idea."

"I haven't changed my mind. I still think it's a great idea."

"Bryce—"

"You owe me a dinner," he pressed.

She didn't, of course. Yet she didn't call him on that fine point. Instead, she groped for something to say that would diffuse the heat that continued to connect them.

"I know a great restaurant."

She did need to talk to him about Nancy, now that Nancy had agreed to see him. Still, that wasn't reason enough to go against everything inside her that told her to say no and mean it.

"You'll need to unwind after your show, so I thought tomorrow night would be perfect."

Perfect?

She wanted to giggle hysterically at such a ludicrous thought. Nothing about them was perfect. Yet she was weakening by the second.

"Are you game?"

"How 'bout I cook dinner for you?"

He seemed taken aback. "You don't have to do that."

"I know, but going out following a hard day at the shop doesn't appeal to me."

"We can make it another day."

She heard the disappointment in his tone which both electrified her and frightened her, a lethal combination where she was concerned.

"Be here at eight."

With that she hung up the receiver, feeling as if she'd just taken a plunge off that mental edge she'd been teetering on since she first saw him.

Eleven

At least he'd gotten his foot back in the door. After the other night, he feared she would never talk to him again. She had been so uptight, downright angry actually, when his cell phone had rung and he'd had to go.

Until then she'd been in rare form, shaking her flame-red hair about her face and grinning devilishly from time to time.

But after that call she had turned cold and unresponsive, as though she were suddenly revolted by him. That change in attitude had dealt him quite a wallop, making him wonder if he'd fooled himself into thinking that there was "something" between them.

Now, however, he felt better, back on a little steadier ground, although with someone who was as volatile as Katherine, one never knew what was going to happen next. That was part of her charm.

He smiled as he kicked back in his chair at the office, thinking of their conversation. For a second he'd gotten her goat when he'd mentioned coming to the trunk show. His eyes suddenly drifted to the invitation in front of him.

He wondered if Katherine herself was going to model any of those frothy garments.

Just thinking about that turned him on, and his libido responded accordingly, forcing him to change positions to relieve the discomfort behind his zipper. Good Lord, but he was a mess.

Still, he was anticipating seeing her that evening. He eyed his sermon notes on his desk and knew he should be concentrating on them, not Katherine.

But she had bewitched him from the first moment she'd walked into the hardware store, her upthrust breasts, great legs and luscious hips swaying in perfect rhythm.

Had he ever felt this way about Molly? He was sure that he had, but it seemed so long ago that he couldn't recall any of those tumultuous feelings. But Katherine—she was a different matter altogether. She absolutely sizzled, and in turn made him sizzle.

Suddenly irritated with his thoughts, Bryce lunged out of the chair and walked to the window. The morning sun was bright and the air outside cool and crisp.

A perfect day for making love in front of the fire-place.

He could understand how easy it would be to curse. Sometime he wished he could. For him that wasn't the answer. While he was a minister who tried to speak and live God's word as best he could, he was still a man with human needs and desires.

And he needed Katherine Mays. He *wanted* Katherine Mays. In his bed. Bryce sucked in a deep breath, then forced it out as he lifted his head and stared at the sky as if searching for help.

None seemed forthcoming, at least not that he was hearing, which increased his frustration. He didn't need this aggravation in his life right now, especially not when the church was about to embark on an aggressive building program. All his efforts and time should be buried in his work, in seeing that the Lord's will was carried out.

Yet he couldn't control how he felt. Yes, he could, he told himself with brutal honesty. Only he didn't want to. He wanted to be with Katherine. He wanted to savor her rich personality and her strong beauty. She was like a brush fire inside him that had gotten out of control.

At the same time, though, he had to face the fact that the fire could burn him badly. Suddenly he recoiled at that thought. Molly's death had hit him hard, and it had taken what seemed like eons for him to bounce back. If it hadn't been for his faith, he didn't think he could've made it.

But he was alive and at the moment wanted to

spend time with Katherine. But what if she wasn't interested? What if she merely wanted him as a friend?

Friend.

He almost choked on that thought. He couldn't exactly nail down that look in her eye, but it was definitely more than friendly. On the conservative side, he'd say there was guarded interest. On the liberal side, he'd say there was some fire in her belly, as well.

Love?

Where did that fit into the scheme of things? It didn't. When he thought about her, he thought about sex, nothing more, nothing less.

His wild thoughts brought a sudden twist to his lips. He hadn't been this foolhardy, this loose in so long he'd forgotten how it felt. He had none other than one wild redhead to thank for that.

A divorced redhead to boot.

Some of his enthusiasm faded, only to rebound when he refused to dwell on that. Her past was something that couldn't be changed. It didn't matter, anyway. It wasn't as if he were going to fall in love with her and marry her. Heck no, he wasn't.

He just wanted to be with her, to share some of her zest for life. And he wouldn't apologize to anyone for doing so. He'd just have to be careful. He'd always been a private person and the fact that he served the Lord and His people didn't mean that he couldn't have a life of his own.

And secrets.

For now Katherine Mays was going to be his best-kept secret. He grinned just as the phone jangled on his desk.

Having been granted a reprieve from his thoughts, Bryce grabbed it on the third ring.

"Ah, Lee Ann, it's good to hear from you. And you're right, we do have a lot to talk about."

Everything was ready or as ready as it was going to be. Katherine's critical eye surveyed the table that was set with cheery place mats and pottery. It was the fresh flowers that adorned the middle that caught her breath. Stargazer lilies. They were her favorite, and lucky for her the florist had just gotten in a fresh shipment that morning.

Was that some kind of omen?

She quickly brushed that thought aside. She vowed to keep the dinner an innocent affair. No more erotic thoughts about the preacher.

So what were they going to talk about? They still had nothing in common. That hadn't changed. Suddenly Katherine's thoughts brightened. Nancy. They could discuss her friend and her needs. After all, hadn't that been the real reason she'd invited him?

If the conversation began to bog down, there was always the church and the building program. Yet she was hesitant to bring that up, as she wasn't sure she was going to go through with the project, Lee Ann or no Lee Ann.

Enough already.

If she didn't stop her mental babbling, she'd be a

basket case by the time Bryce arrived. Speaking of arriving, her gaze went to the clock, and she noticed he should be there any moment.

With her heart beating more rapidly than usual, she walked into the bedroom and stood in front of the full-length mirror for one last perusal.

Not bad, she mused.

She had chosen a hot-pink silk jumpsuit. The color should've fought with her coloring but it didn't. She thought it made her hair and skin look that much more vibrant. She wondered what *he* would think.

Aw, to heck with that, she told herself. Once this dinner was over, no more personal encounters. This evening would be a piece of cake. She smiled suddenly, thinking of the cake she'd baked.

She didn't know what had come over her, but she'd gotten out her mother's hot-chocolate cake recipe and made it. However, the deli was supplying the rest of the meal, which was chicken gumbo, salad and hot bread.

The smell coming from the kitchen was yummy, calling attention to the fact that she hadn't eaten all day. But then she hadn't had time.

The doorbell chimed. Ignoring her rising heartbeat, she hurried to open it.

"Hey," he said, holding out a bouquet of flowers.

Katherine was slightly taken aback. The guys she'd dated lately would never have been so thoughtful. But then, Bryce was a different breed altogether, which made him more dangerous. She must keep that in mind.

"Why, thanks," she said, taking them and gesturing for him to come in.

He paused in the middle of the living room and looked around. "Mmm, nice place you have here."

"Thanks," she murmured, thinking how nice *he* looked in slacks that hugged his legs, and a long-sleeved knit shirt that did the same to his stomach, showing off his flat, tight muscles. He smelled wonderful, the scent of his cologne rivaling the flowers in her arms.

"Ah, I see you already have some posies," he commented, smiling.

She returned his smile, though she avoided his eyes. "Now we'll have posies for the living room."

"That'll work."

"Please, sit down and I'll get you something to drink."

"Hey, you don't have to wait on me. You sit, and I'll take care of the drinks. I bet I can find my way around."

She smiled, then shrugged her shoulders. "All right."

Moments later he came back with two cups of flavored decaf coffee and napkins, taking a seat on the other end of the sofa from her.

For a moment they sipped in silence, watching the fire sizzle.

"So how did the show go?" he asked, his gaze wandering over her. "I thought about you."

For no reason at all, she flushed. Dammit, she had

to stop doing that. But how, when those eyes seemed to undress her, and with no apology, either?

"Great, but I'm exhausted."

"I can see it in your eyes. That's why you should've let me take you out." He paused. "Though I have to admit this is much better."

"I'm hungry," she said, rising, dodging those smoldering eyes again. "How 'bout you?"

He stood, picking up both cups. "Woman, I'm always hungry, especially when whatever's cooking smells delicious."

To her surprise, Katherine was totally relaxed during the meal. But then, the temperature between them was normal. He made her laugh with stories about some of his experiences when he was a youth minister. She shared with him humorous comments and events that she'd encountered in the retail business.

"I guess everyone has their favorite war stories," he said, as they made their way back into the living room, only after he'd insisted on cleaning up the kitchen.

"You don't have to do that," she'd said, appalled.

"I want to. And I'm a mean cleaner."

Now as they faced each other once again on the sofa, an uninvited tension seemed to invade the room. Before it got further out of hand, Katherine said, "My friend Nancy's agreed to talk to you."

Bryce's eyebrows rose. "Are you serious?"

"Yes, so don't blow it."

He pitched back his head and laughed. "Why don't you just say what's on your mind?"

She gave him a sheepish smile. "I think I just did."

"And I like that."

Silence.

"In fact, I like you." Suddenly the timbre of his voice changed as did the look in his eyes. *Hot* was the word that came to mind.

The air in the room suddenly compressed. "Bryce—"

"Sorry, that wasn't what I meant to say."

She should've been relieved at his apology, but she wasn't. Damn, what did she want from this man? That was the problem—she didn't know. And that was what scared her the most.

"Apology accepted," she said, playing nervously with the gold chain around her neck.

"I have to ask you something."

She was instantly suspicious, yet she nodded in the affirmative.

"Why did you get so angry the other night when my cell phone rang?"

"You know I've been married." Her words were a flat statement of fact.

He didn't so much as flinch. "I know."

"Well, he was a politician, a congressman from another district. Did you know that, too?"

"No."

Lee Ann had continued to hold her tongue. Good girl. "Like you he belonged to the people he served, his constituents."

"Ah, and that bothered you?"

She laughed, minus the humor. "Big-time. He

wanted me to be the consummate congressman's wife, beholden to the people as well. More than that, he wanted to control me, wanted me at his beck and call twenty-four hours a day, seven days a week.''

Bryce frowned. ''He doesn't sound like a very nice man. I'm assuming he's still around.''

''Very much so, but he doesn't bother me.''

''That's good.''

''I was only twenty-two, fresh out of college, when I met him. He was already a first-term congressman who was not only wealthy but who had a high profile.''

''And he swept you off your feet.''

''I guess you could say that, though I went into my marriage with the intention of making it work. But...'' Her voice faded and she peered down at her hands that were clenched tightly in her lap.

''So what went wrong?'' His tone was gentle.

''Look, I'd rather not talk about this anymore,'' she said abruptly, realizing she was about to spill her guts. ''I've said far too much as it is.''

Bryce didn't say anything for the longest time. He simply looked at her with unreadable eyes. Although she wanted to avoid them, she couldn't. For some reason she found sympathy and comfort there.

''He was a fool.'' His tone was low and slightly cracked. ''For more reasons than one, I would imagine.''

Katherine's mouth went dry as she stared into his eyes that burned with intensity. ''Please, I told you I don't want to discuss me or my past anymore.''

"No problem," he said on a much lighter note.

"So how 'bout you? Were you happily married?"

"Absolutely."

She pushed aside a stab of envy and said, "Lucky you."

"Yes, I was. But for some reason the Lord had better plans for her."

"Other than the heartbreak of losing her, any regrets at all?"

"Yeah, not having children. Molly and I thought we had all the time in the world. But I was just starting out in church work as a youth minister and even with Molly working, we had very little money coming in."

When she didn't respond right off, he went on, "If your marriage had been different, would you have had children?"

"No."

His eyebrows shot up. She knew she'd shocked him with her blunt sincerity, but that couldn't be helped. That was the way she felt.

"No curtain climbers for you, huh?"

His lips were twitching in that special way of his which eased the unsettled atmosphere a bit.

"That's right. I'm a free spirit who wants to be accountable to no one."

Bryce inclined his head. "I think I'll let that one slide for the moment."

She grinned. "That shocks you, doesn't it?"

"Nothing shocks me anymore, but—" Bryce stopped, then batted the air. "Ah, forget it."

She did, not wanting to step any deeper into that personal arena. It would accomplish nothing, except to highlight the differences between them.

"I can't tell you how much I appreciate your agreeing to help Lee Ann. I think you'll be a prize asset."

For some unexplainable and invalid reason, Katherine felt miffed, wondering if his push to see her stemmed from her talent rather than her personally.

"Oh, really?"

Unexpectedly he moved closer, his eyes darkening. "I'm not using you, you have to know that."

Color bathed her cheeks. Had he read her mind? That would never do. "Look, I didn't mean—"

"It doesn't matter," Bryce countered in a husky tone. "My motive for coming here was purely selfish."

Her pulse rate soared as his breath mingled with hers. She wanted to pull back, but she was powerless against the force of his attraction.

"And if I don't touch you right now, I can't make it another second."

Startled, her lips parted, and that was when he claimed them in a deep, melting kiss that affected her clear down to her toes. Then he pulled back and stared at her, looking more startled than she felt, as if he'd just been hit by an oncoming train.

"Bryce." She barely got the word out.

"If you expect me to apologize, you can forget it," he said in a strangled voice.

"I—"

Further words were jammed in her throat as he took her lips again, this time in quiet desperation.

Twelve

So he'd kissed her.

So she'd let her guard slip. It wasn't the end of the freaking world. Therefore, she should stop beating up on herself. She should just give him and the kiss a rest.

However, that was easier said than done, she was finding out the following Monday afternoon, several days after the incident.

Katherine shook her head as if to clear it, then turned back to the invoices spread across her desk. Even though the store was closed, Nancy had come down for a few hours to help her unpack more freight and to get organized for the week.

Katherine's was having a red-tag sale beginning

midweek and everything had to be marked. They had made headway toward that when Nancy had had to leave.

She had an appointment with Bryce—her first. Although Katherine felt anxious about the outcome of that meeting, she was nonetheless confident that she had done the right thing in getting them together.

Nancy certainly needed help. Neither she nor her family could afford to pay for it. So far, though, Wally had left her and the kids alone. If Nancy could get herself straight, get over the idea that it was her fault that Wally struck her, then she'd be on her way to recovery.

It wasn't an easy feat. She knew: she'd been there and done that. Suddenly she shuddered, then grew angry. Rarely did she let the darkness from the past spill into the sunlight of today. Her employee's present plight had something to do with that, she knew. Still, dredging up memories from a sordid past was nothing she intended to dwell on for long.

Pouring herself another cup of hot tea, she parked herself back at the table and began perusing the invoices. After a few moments when all the figures bled together, she made a growling sound in her throat and pushed the papers away.

Edgy.

That was the word that fit her. And *hyper.* The two of them together made for another lethal combination just like her and Bryce. Damn him. Why did he have to kiss her? Why did she *let* him kiss her? She was as responsible as he was—actually more so.

She had seen it coming and could have stopped it. But she hadn't, not even the second time when his tongue had invaded her mouth and she'd clung to him as if she'd never let him go.

She groaned. But the memory of how his lips felt on hers, sending that rush of hot adrenaline through her system, made her ache for more.

That was why she was in trouble. Bryce wasn't like all her other men, whom she could take or leave at a moment's notice. If she never heard from any of them again, she wouldn't miss a beat. Her philosophy had always been that if any man got close enough to kiss her, they were *too* close. She wanted men as friends, not lovers.

But again, Bryce was a different breed altogether, she admitted with another groan. She hadn't wanted to let him go, only she hadn't let him know that. That was her one saving grace.

After he'd kissed her that second time, she'd jerked out of his arms and struggled for a decent breath.

"This shouldn't happen again," she'd finally said when she was coherent.

"I don't see why not. We're both grown, consenting adults."

"That's a given, but we're on a dead-end street."

"If that's the case," he said with smoldering ease, "then we can always turn around and head back the other way."

"Funny."

He chuckled and touched her face again. She pulled

back, and for a second his lips tightened. "I want to see you again. And again."

"I don't want to see you." Her eyes flashed and her tone was belligerent.

"Liar," he said in a strained whisper.

Now, as she placed the palm of her hands against her hot cheeks, she felt mortified all over again. But dammit, she didn't want to want him. He would always put someone else ahead of her. She didn't want to play second fiddle again.

And a preacher. Worst-case scenario. She was no more suited to becoming involved with a man of the cloth than a streetwalker was. Suddenly she sighed, picturing his congregation's reaction if they were to get wind of what was going on. They would have a conniption fit.

No matter. Even if he had nipped their relationship in the bud, it still wouldn't be wise to help Lee Ann. Although her path and Bryce's might not cross all that much, she couldn't take a chance on that.

She had to get out while the getting was good, even if she had to take the chicken's way out. With that not-so-nice thought in mind, she reached for the phone.

"Hey, it's me," she said.

"I was about to call you," Lee Ann said.

"What's up?"

"Can you be at the church in a little while? I guess you could say we're about to have our first official meeting."

"I want you to find someone else. I just don't think—"

"Now, you listen here, Katherine Mays, you promised," Lee Ann said in a heated but loving tone. "And I'm not about to let you weasel out." She paused only long enough to take a deep breath. "Besides, I have a bone to pick with you."

Thrown momentarily off track, Katherine asked, "And just what might that be?"

"*People* are talking."

Katherine's heart dropped to her toes. Were her thoughts about to bear fruit? Oh, Lordy. Still, she played the innocent. "People are always talking."

"But not about you and Bryce." Lee Ann's tone was coated in syrup.

Katherine's stomach revolted. "How did—"

"Not to worry. I'll tell you all about it when I see you shortly."

"Lee Ann!"

"Later."

"Don't you dare hang up on me!"

The line went dead. She cursed, but it didn't make her feel any better. So the gossipmongers were already out beating their tom-toms. But who had given them the fodder? How on earth had they found out she was seeing Bryce?

Had seen Bryce, she corrected herself. It was important that she think of him in the past tense.

She hadn't a clue who had spotted them, but no doubt she would find out. What to do? That was the question. If she didn't show up at the meeting, Lee

Ann would kill her. If she *did* show up, she would see Bryce.

Which fate did she fear the worse?

"So, ladies, it looks to me like you have everything under control."

"Lee Ann has everything under control, don't you mean?" Katherine knew her tone was churlish, but she didn't care.

Bryce's only reaction was to quirk an eyebrow, then smile at the two of them with a glint in his eye. Katherine forced herself to turn away from that smile, which brightened his face like a hundred-watt bulb, thus making him that much more attractive.

The instant she had walked into his office and he'd stood, the room had seemed to shrink. Or maybe it had been the way he'd looked at her, his eyes making a deliberate and disturbing sweep of her entire body.

Her breath had hung suspended while all her good intentions of holding strong against his pull seemed to melt along with her insides. Somehow, though, she had managed to get control and give him a cool smile.

She had managed to hang on to that coolness until now, until that "smile" seemed to hit another raw spot. She lowered her head so that he or Lee Ann wouldn't see the color that invaded her cheeks.

"Don't mind my friend here," Lee Ann said, grinning. "She can't help it. She just got up on the wrong side of the bed this morning."

Katherine cut her a look, though she smiled. "Cute."

She might as well get off her high horse. After all, she had shown up for the meeting and had even made several suggestions that had been well received. Finally Lee Ann had brought things to a close, and they were about to leave.

"Thanks, ladies," Bryce was saying. "We're off to a great start, especially with the offices."

"I think so, too," Lee Ann said. "Once we get you and the other staffers taken care of, we'll start on the parlor."

"Works for me," Bryce said.

Lee Ann snapped her briefcase shut. "If there's nothing else, then I'm out of here."

"Me, too." Katherine stood.

Bryce opened his mouth as if to speak, only to have the phone ring. He excused himself, answered it, then placed his hand over the receiver. "Katherine, I'll only be a second. Would you mind hanging around a minute?"

Katherine gave a start, but when she looked at him, his features were bland and innocent. Innocent be damned. He knew exactly what he was doing.

"All right," she conceded, but not graciously.

Once she and Lee Ann were out in the secretary's office, Lee Ann started in, "I'm hurt that you didn't confide in me."

"There's nothing to confide, for heaven's sake," Katherine hissed.

"Ha, there was enough high-volume electricity in that room to break a rich man."

Katherine glared at her.

"Every time he looked at you, and that was a lot, he seemed to be devouring you."

"Oh, get real," Katherine shot back.

"Tell me how long you've been seeing him?"

Katherine barely curbed her growing frustration. "Who told you?"

Lee Ann gave her an impish smile. "No one."

Relief rocked Katherine, leaving her weak in the knees. "Then how—"

"I just happened to drive by and see his car at your house."

"So the gossipmongers aren't running amok?"

"Nope."

"Thank God."

"I'm waiting." Lee Ann's impish grin was still in place.

Katherine fought the urge to grab her friend and shake the daylights out of her, but she didn't. "I invited him to dinner to discuss Nancy, who'd decided she wanted his help. That's all. Now are you happy?"

She hated lying, and in the church, no less, but it couldn't be helped. Some things she just couldn't share, and her feelings for Bryce were one of them.

Lee Ann's grin faded. "I guess. I was just hoping for more."

Katherine ruffled Lee Ann's hair, then said pointedly, "Forget it. Take your rear home."

"See you later, then," Lee Ann said with a downward turn to her mouth.

Before Katherine could gather her scattered wits

about her, Bryce walked out. "Is it about Nancy?" she asked.

"What about her?"

"Did she keep her appointment?"

"That she did."

"I was afraid she hadn't and that's what you wanted to see me about."

"Actually, Nancy had nothing to do with it."

"Oh," she said inanely.

His eyes fell to her mouth, then came back to her eyes. "I'm about to take my friend's plane for a spin. I want you to go with me."

Thirteen

"**I**'m worthless now."

Doris Burnette gave her son a teasing smile at the same time a mischievous warmth appeared in her eye. "Only now?"

Bryce gave her a look.

She chuckled, then sat down in her recliner across from the sofa where Bryce had sprawled after consuming more food than he had in a while.

He stared at his mother and massaged his stomach. "Man, but those were good peas and cornbread. The best."

"You say that every time."

"And the peach cobbler, it *was* the best."

"Don't worry, the peaches won't run out. I put plenty of bags in the freezer."

"Good girl."

Doris merely shook her head as she stared at her son with an indulgent look on her face. "I like seeing you eat well. It's a good sign."

"I don't know so much about that." Bryce rubbed his belly harder. "If I chowed down like this often, I'd have to hit the jogging track every day."

"You're perfect just the way you are. Besides, you're like your daddy. You can eat all you want and never gain an ounce." She paused and grimaced. "Now, me, I just look at food and put on weight."

"Baloney. I think you're pretty much perfect the way you are."

That twinkle jumped back into her eyes. "You're just prejudiced, but I'm glad."

They fell silent for a moment. Bryce watched his mother go to work with her knitting needles before turning his attention to the gas logs burning brightly in the small fireplace.

But it wasn't the fire that danced before his eyes but images of Katherine. Stifling a groan, he closed his eyes and took several deep breaths. He didn't want to think about her. He wanted to continue to relax and enjoy the remainder of the evening with his mother.

This privilege didn't come his way often. He was always too busy taking care of his flock, even during his off time. *Off time.* Ha, that was a joke. His time was never his own. Katherine was right about that.

However, every once in a while he got lucky. To-night was one of those times. And he had taken full advantage of both the splendid meal and the warm conversation that Doris offered.

"Tired, huh?"

He smiled as he stretched. "Always."

"When are you going to slow down?"

"Never."

"If I told you you needed to, you wouldn't pay me any mind, would you?"

"No, ma'am," Bryce drawled.

She gave him a reprimanding look, then her features cleared. "Are you about ready for another cup of coffee?"

"I'll get it."

"You'll do no such thing." Doris put her knitting down and got up. "I love waiting on you. I'm honored that you chose me over flying the plane." Her lips twitched. "For once, that is."

Bryce winced, then watched her back as she headed for the kitchen. That wince was followed by a niggling guilt. The truth was, he hadn't chosen her over flying. He'd had every intention of going for a joyride, only his plans hadn't worked out.

Katherine. She was the reason.

Her image leaped back to mind, recalling the conversation they'd had after their meeting. When he'd asked her to go with him, she hadn't hesitated.

"No," she'd said.

"No? Just like that?"

"I don't fly in small planes."

He didn't bother to mask his disappointment, having envisioned them flying high and laughing out loud as he guided the plane through the sky. "That's too bad."

"I'd rather not fly the big jets, but I do out of necessity because I love to travel."

"Is it a control thing?"

He could see that he'd struck a raw nerve by the way her eyes suddenly sparked. "I guess you might say that."

He forced a grin. "I'm in control, at least while I'm piloting."

"Unfortunately, that's not good enough." She tempered her words with a smile.

He stared at her a moment longer, then nodded. "I guess I have no choice but to accept that."

"I guess you don't." She hesitated, then added, "I'll see you later."

With that she had walked off, the sway of her hips remaining with him long after he got in his car. Frustrated with anger and need, he had come straight to his mother's, where he'd done some chores around the house while she prepared dinner.

"My, but you look serious."

Startled out of his reverie, Bryce reached for the cup Doris held out to him and took a sip. The liquid burned all the way down, but he hardly noticed, his insides already singed from his minor clash with Katherine.

"What's wrong?"

He hadn't realized he'd registered his feelings visibly until he saw Doris's frown of concern. "Nothing."

"I know better," she chastised mildly. "In fact, you've been a bit distracted all evening." She paused. "Are you already having problems with the building program?"

"Not so far, but I'm not off the hook yet. You know there's opposition."

"There's always that. It's impossible to please all the people all the time. But from the vote, you've pleased the majority."

"And I feel thankful for that, believe me."

"Then what is it? What has you down in the mouth?" She gave him another of her teasing smiles. "I know it's not a woman."

"Actually, it is," he blurted out, then wanted to kick his rear.

Her eyes widened, and her needles stopped clicking, creating a sudden and complete silence in the room. "You mean you're interested in someone?"

His mother sounded so shocked that he had to smile, though it was short-lived. "Yes."

"Does she go to our church?"

"No."

"But she does attend church somewhere?"

"Not regularly, I'm sorry to say."

Doris's features were grave. "Oh, dear."

"Before you go getting in a dither, it's nothing serious. It's just that—" His voice trailed off for lack of a way to express himself. He hadn't meant to talk about Katherine.

Where she was concerned, his feelings were so scrambled that he couldn't figure them out himself, much less explain to someone else, least of all his mother.

Yet he'd opened his big mouth and spilled his guts. But then maybe deep down he'd wanted her opinion. After all, she was a sage old woman who'd always had her head on straight.

"Who is she, son?" Doris said into the silence.

"It's Katherine Mays who owns Katherine's."

She gave him an incredulous stare. "That lingerie and dress shop?"

"One in the same."

"Oh, Bryce, I don't even know what to say."

"Turns out she's a friend of Lee Ann's who's agreed to help with the decorating."

"I see."

"You don't approve."

"Does it matter?" she asked softly.

"Of course it does."

"Then I'd advise you to run like a scalded dog. She's not at all what you need in a wife. Molly—"

"Molly's dead, Mother." The instant he said that, he felt like a heel, but he couldn't recall the words. The damage had been done.

She changed positions in the chair. "You said it wasn't serious."

"Only because it won't work, because we're from two different worlds."

"Oh, son, please be careful. You've worked so hard to get where you are now. I'd hate to see you lose it all."

"And you think my seeing Katherine could cause that?"

"Let's just say I'm afraid for you."

He crossed the room and kissed her on the cheek. "Don't be. I'll never do anything to make you ashamed of me."

"That could never happen." She squinted up at him once again. "Angry, yes. Ashamed, no." Suddenly that twinkle appeared back in her eye. "At least you'll give some of those old biddies something to talk about."

He laughed, then sobered. "I promise I'll get my head back on straight. Just give me a little time."

"Be careful, son. That's all I ask." She smiled. "Now, finish your coffee, then go home. This old woman needs her beauty rest."

Bryce noticed the lights on in the shop before he saw her car. He made a face. What was she doing working at this hour of the night? Simple. Like him she probably had more to do than she could get done during the day.

Still, that didn't sit well with him. It wasn't safe. At least that was the excuse he used to whip his utility vehicle into the parking lot. He didn't get out right away, calling himself a fool for pursuing her and this relationship.

But that gnawing in his gut made him reach for the handle and jerk it open. Seconds later he was tapping on the glass, thinking he would probably frighten her out of her wits.

"Who is it?" she asked, just as another light turned on.

He could hear the slight tremor in her voice and wished now he'd ignored that craving to see her, *to touch her,* and kept right on going.

A cold shower could work miracles.

"Bryce, what on earth?" She unlocked the door, her eyes wide with dismay. "Is something wrong?"

"No."

"Then why are you here?"

He shrugged. "I was worried."

She gave him a suspicious look. "About me?"

"Yep."

"Right."

He cleared his throat. "May I come in?"

"Give me one good reason why I should let you."

His eyes burned into hers. "Because you want to see me as much as I want to see you," he said roughly. He'd thrown that out there for whatever it was worth, having no idea how she'd take it.

Wild color surged into her face, and her eyes widened. But she didn't deny it. Instead she stepped aside. "Follow me," she said, then turned and headed toward the back.

"Ah, this is cozy," he said, once they reached the room that obviously served as office, kitchen and storage. Boxes were everywhere. No wonder she was working.

"Don't you mean crowded?" she said, facing him, a hint of a smile softening her lips.

"That, too."

"Would you like something to drink?"

She was looking at him through those big, gorgeous brown eyes that were underlined with dusty circles. "No, thanks. What I would like is for you to go home."

"Bryce—"

He heard the frustration in her voice, but that didn't stop him from stepping closer. She swallowed and stepped back, though her gaze didn't waver.

"Bryce, what?" he asked thickly.

She straightened her spine. "You really shouldn't be here."

"I know."

"I just want us to be friends."

"We are." He couldn't take his eyes off her mouth, especially that plump lower lip, more moist and inviting than ever. He knew how it tasted and that was the problem.

"Then don't come any closer. Please." That last word was barely audible.

"I can't help it."

Although he knew he was disturbing her, her gaze didn't waver. "I don't mean as kissing friends," she said, her voice quavering.

He wondered how she would react if he touched her breasts, thumbed a tempting nipple, visible against her clinging shirt. "What makes you think I'm about to kiss you?"

"Aren't you?" That quaver again.

"God, yes."

He grabbed her then and sank his lips onto hers.

At first she resisted. But when he was greedily relentless with the pressure, they opened suddenly like a flower to the sun. He moaned, drinking in their sweetness, feeling his head spin.

But he didn't stop there. A hand slipped under her long-sleeved T-shirt and surrounded a burgeoning breast. Her bra was of no consequence as the clasp in front was easily undone.

When her breasts were freed and he felt the soft flesh against his callused palm, another moan surfaced. It was only after he had backed her against the wall and pressed his hardness against her stomach that she made a sound.

Her whimper tore at him, brought him to his senses. He jerked back and stared down into her liquid eyes.

"This time I will apologize," he ground out, desperately trying to regain control of his splattered emotions.

She crossed her arms around her chest as if to stop herself from trembling. "Apology accepted," she whispered.

He reached out and pushed several strands of hair out of her face. "What is there about you, Katherine Mays," he whispered, "that makes me do crazy things?"

"I wish I knew, and I'd stop doing them."

Her attempt at humor saved the moment, saved him from making a bigger fool of himself than he already had. He forced a smile and stepped back out of harm's way, though that was one of the hardest steps he'd ever taken.

And his body rebelled as well. He was so hard and so hot that it was all he could do not to clear that table with their bodies, jerk her clothes off and bury himself deep inside her.

As if she could read his mind, her face became more flushed, and that tremor reappeared in her voice. "Bryce, this can't go on or we'll both do something stupid."

His eyes darkened, and he expelled a shuddering breath. "Like make love?"

"Yes," she said simply, once again running her tongue across her now-swollen lower lip.

That gesture added to his misery, yet he couldn't seem to let it go, let her go. "Would that be so terrible?"

"Bryce—"

"Sorry, forget I asked that." He paused. "You're not going to stop working on the project, are you?"

She was quiet for a moment, then tilted her head up at him. "Only if you promise not to touch me again."

"I promise," he said, releasing a harsh breath.

Her breathing seemed to be easier, however, when she said, "Then I suggest you head home."

He made a sweeping gesture with a hand. "Ladies first."

"Oh, all right."

A few minutes later, watching her taillights disappear, Bryce had never felt more lonely or out of control in his life. Slowly he lifted his eyes heavenward.

Fourteen

"How did your session go? Or should I say sessions?"

Nancy's pale features suddenly brightened. "Really well."

"You sound surprised," Katherine said.

Nancy shrugged. "I was dreading meeting with Bryce, I'll admit. But he's cool, just the dose of tonic I needed."

"Believe me, I'm grateful that you went and thankful that it's working."

Nancy didn't respond for a moment, watching Katherine as she moved a handful of glittery dresses from one rack to the other. "I think Wally may go and talk to him, too."

Katherine paused, but only for a moment. "Do you think that's smart, seeing Wally again, I mean?"

Nancy's face crumpled. "No, but I love him."

"What did Bryce say about that?" The moment the words left her mouth, she held up her hand. "You don't have to tell me that. You have to make your own decisions. I have no right to judge."

"Yes, you do." Nancy gave her a wan smile. "You've put up with my whining and everything else. As for Bryce, he doesn't know I'm even talking to my husband again."

Katherine stifled a sigh. "Are you going to tell him?"

"Yes, even if Wally reneges."

"Good. He'll be able to advise you. I just want you to be careful. Wally's hurt you too much already."

"I know."

Katherine forced a smile. "We'd best get the lead out of our panties and finish moving these racks and clothes before the masses hit."

Nancy rolled her eyes. "Don't we hope."

The buzzer sounded, and Katherine grinned, then winked. "Go girl. You're on this morning. If you need me, holler."

Nancy groaned good-naturedly, then scurried out of the back.

Once she was alone, Katherine took a sip of Coke and looked around at the office. For once what she saw didn't frighten her. The sale was in full swing, and so far the shop had done great. She had gotten rid of a lot of dresses that had been around too long, dresses that had been shoved from the back to the front countless times.

She was sick of looking at them. There were a few pieces of lingerie that fitted into that same category. Now both were history. Some lucky or unlucky ladies were now the proud owners.

More than anything, though, she had made money, money that she would manage to put back in the company, her heart still set on opening another store.

However, she had enough on her plate to digest at the moment without even thinking about expanding. She swallowed another sigh, mentally berating herself for letting her heart overrule her head and committing to Lee Ann and that church project.

It wasn't that the project wasn't a fun challenge. She loved challenges, especially when it came to turning something not so lovely into something magnificent.

But she'd suspected it was too time consuming, and it placed her directly in Brycc's line of fire. If only the offices hadn't been first on the agenda, then maybe she wouldn't be in such a mental and physical snit.

Katherine tapped her pencil on the table, letting her mind go where it wanted, which was back to Bryce. She laughed a hollow laugh. Who was she kidding? She didn't have to be around Bryce to think about him. Her thoughts *stayed* on him. She'd begun to think he'd taken up permanent residence in her mind.

But what about her heart? Had he managed to sneak in there, as well?

Posing those questions quickened her breath. She had worked so hard to keep her heart from becoming exposed to Bryce and his magical charm. But she was afraid with each passing day that her immunity to him was weakening.

"Damn," she muttered, slamming the pencil down and flexing her shoulders.

The day was just getting started, and here she was fixating on him. But that last visit and kiss in this very room had just about sent her over the edge.

If he hadn't pulled back, would she have let him make love to her? Yes. She had to admit that, a truth she could no longer deny and face herself in the mirror.

So what did that mean? Had she gone and done something stupid like fallen in love? No! Of course not. What she felt for him was lust. There. Now that she jerked that admission out of the darkest corner of her mind, she felt better.

But it didn't solve her problem. She still didn't want to be attracted to him. She still didn't want to need him. She still didn't want to want him. And every time she was with him, those "wants" deepened.

Yet they could have no permanent relationship. Even if they were both willing, it wouldn't work. She flatly refused to live with another man who was beholden to others.

So why didn't she tell him to leave her alone and

mean it? For one thing he wouldn't take no for an answer. And he did it with such disarming charm that she was snookered before she realized it.

Several times during the past few weeks, when she'd been at the church going through countless piles of fabric and wallpaper books and furniture catalogs, she'd been conscious of his presence with every fiber of her being.

His smell toyed with her senses. His smile melted her insides. And his laughter lifted her spirits. Hence, when he'd asked her to dinner or to a movie, she'd capitulated.

But as he promised, he hadn't touched her again. He'd kept things on a friendship basis just the way she'd wanted. And that was the problem. She didn't want that. Suddenly she made a face and moved around in her chair. She wanted to feel his hot, sucking lips on hers again, feel the hungry urgency of his hands on her breasts…

"Yo!"

Katherine jumped as if she'd been shot. "Uh, coming."

She tore out of the room, thanking God for small favors.

"I think we're all done here, Travis."

The assistant minister gathered his papers and stuffed them back into the folder, then stood. "Do you think anything will ever be normal around here again?"

Bryce merely shook his head. "I'm beginning to doubt it."

"Why did we think this was going to be great?" Travis asked, sounding down in the mouth.

"Hey, buck up," Bryce responded, standing. "Eating a little dust is good for the soul."

"Says who?"

Bryce laughed. "Just wait till they start the sanctuary."

"Don't even talk about it. My allergies are already on the warpath."

"I'll see you later."

Travis paused at the door and swung around. "Is it next week you're going to that church conference?"

"Yes, so remind me to go over some things with you at the end of the week. I already have a list, which includes several meetings I want you to attend in my place."

"No problem."

Once Travis had left, Bryce turned and stared out the window, his aim dead center on the land that was being cleared before his eyes. A new place in which to worship, to preach the word of God.

His goal. *His dream.*

Why wasn't he jumping through hoops with joy? Why was he standing there as if he had the weight of the world on his shoulders?

Katherine.

Just thinking about her now, or any other time for that matter, sent a pang of longing through him so sharp it almost bent him double.

Yet when they were together, he had behaved himself. It had taken every ounce of self-discipline he could muster, but he'd kept his promise, though it had taken its toll on his heart and his libido.

But once she'd realized he wasn't going to pounce on her—a cynical smile twisted his lips—then she'd relaxed and seemed to have a great time.

They had discussed everything under the sun except their feelings for each other, of course. Politics. The world situation. Children killing children. Many other things. For the most part their views had coincided, which was a shocker.

When opinions differed, however, the sparks would fly, especially from her, which made him want her that much more. God, she was so wild, so sassy, so intriguing.

So different from Molly.

How could he be so infatuated with someone like that, someone who in no way fitted the mold of a minister's wife? Without warning, his blood turned to ice water despite the fact that the September day was quite warm.

Wife?

Now where had that thought come from? Granted, he wasn't at all happy with not touching and kissing her. He longed to do both. But even that wouldn't be enough to satisfy his appetite for her.

Seeing her constantly made him yearn for more, much more. After having tasted her lips that last time, touched her satin skin, squeezed her plump breast, he'd been in physical agony.

Bryce pounded his right palm with a left fist. The gesture seemed to expel some of the tension building inside him. Yet he couldn't dodge the questions or the self-doubts that pounded his inner soul.

Was what he felt for her merely a physical attraction? Or was it deep-and-abiding love? He began sweating profusely at the thought it might be the latter.

He couldn't be in love with her. *He just couldn't be.*

"Bryce."

He swung around to face his secretary, who hovered in the doorway, staring at him, an odd look of her face.

"Are you all right?" she finally asked, a tentative note in her voice.

"Fine." He made himself smile. "What's up?"

She stepped farther inside and closed the door behind her. "Mrs. Tipperman and Mrs. Vines are here to see you."

"Ah, send them in."

Julie grimaced. "I'm not sure that's a good idea."

"What makes you say that?"

Julie's face turned red. "I heard them talking, and it's not good."

"Well, you don't worry about it. Send 'em in, and I'll soothe their ruffled feathers, no matter what it is."

"All right," Julie said, though she looked doubtful and didn't quite meet his eyes.

A few minutes later the two women were in his office, comfortable in the chairs in front of his desk.

Both had blue hair, though Mrs. Tipperman was the older of the two and the most attractive.

And both had money. Along with their husbands, they bore a lot of the financial burdens of the church.

He smiled. "Ladies, what a pleasure."

No smile in return. No comment. Ouch. Something was up.

He didn't have to wait long to find out, either.

"We didn't know if we should come here or not," Mrs. Tipperman remarked, her thin lips growing thinner.

"You're always welcome," Bryce responded with an easy confidence, hoping to reassure them.

"But we felt we had no choice," Lucille Vines said, "under the circumstances," she added, color rushing into her horse-shaped face.

"And just what circumstances would that be?" Bryce asked in a soft, indulgent tone. These two had always been among his favorites and his biggest supporters. Too, he had the utmost respect for them.

They looked at each other, then back at him.

"I'm listening, ladies."

"It's 'that' woman," Mrs. Vines said in a hushed tone.

"What woman?" Bryce asked with the innocence of a child, though a gong was sounding inside his head, his mother's warning bearing fruit.

"Katherine Mays, that's who." Violet Tipperman's mouth suddenly puckered as if she'd just bitten into a sour grape and been forced to swallow it.

"Ah, I see," Bryce responded.

"No, I don't think you do," Lucille said, "or you wouldn't be seen in public with her."

"Why is that?" Bryce asked calmly, beginning to sympathize with someone who was walking a high-wire without a net.

"For one thing she's divorced," Violet snapped. "For another, she has an unsavory reputation."

Bryce's temper suddenly heated up, but he hung tough. He wasn't about to give them the satisfaction of knowing they had kicked him in the gut.

He pulled himself together and forced a smile. "I appreciate you ladies so much."

Lucille rose to her feet, obviously aghast at his response. "Is that all you have to say?"

"At the moment."

Violet jumped back into the ring. "Well, that isn't all I have to say." Her eyes bore into Bryce. "She's inappropriate for a preacher's wife. With that in mind, we suggest you stop seeing her."

Fifteen

——

"**W**hat's with you lately?"

Katherine gave Lee Ann a pointed look. "You'll have to be more specific than that."

Lee Ann harrumphed. "The hell you say. I'm your best friend, remember?"

"So?" Katherine teased.

"So I can read you like a book."

"Well, in this case you're on the wrong page," Katherine stressed, though with not as much conviction in her voice as she would have liked. She was afraid she knew exactly what Lee Ann was referring to, but she wasn't ready to admit it.

"The heck I am," Lee Ann responded. "You've been moping around like a sick puppy."

"Thanks."

"You have, and you know it," Lee Ann said, brooking no argument. "Too, you haven't been going out. After you moved back to town, you kicked up your heels every weekend with a different man." Lee Ann paused briefly. "Now, all of a sudden, you're not seeing anyone—except Bryce, that is."

Lee Ann *had* turned to the correct page, and Katherine realized she was in trouble. Her friend wouldn't let go until she got to the bottom of what was gnawing at Katherine.

Lee Ann had stopped by Katherine's house, bringing with her a new book of fabrics, as none had been suitable in the others. So they were having to start back at square one.

It was a chilly, rainy day, atypical for September and perfect for staying inside. Because it was Monday, Katherine had decided to do just that. The sale had ended at the shop, and it had been successful far beyond her wildest expectations. People she'd never seen before were grabbing items off the racks like crazy.

But she was tired and didn't feel guilty about taking a real day off, from paperwork and all. Of course, there was her obligation to the church, but that wasn't really work. She had begun to see it as a labor of love for her friend, and to her surprise she was enjoying it.

And the best part about it was that it kept her in close contact with Bryce.

She groaned.

"Hey, are you sick? Is that what your moping's all about?" Lee Ann's face and voice were filled with concern, the earlier humor no longer in evidence.

"No, silly, I'm not sick."

"Well, you just groaned."

"You don't miss anything, do you?"

"No."

Katherine laughed, realizing she hadn't done much of that the past week, the week that Bryce had been gone.

"Are you going to tell me why you're not partying anymore? Or do I have to guess?"

"Lee Ann, let it go, please," Katherine pleaded, feeling the panic rising inside her.

"It's Bryce, isn't it?" Lee Ann exclaimed, her eyes probing.

"You're not going to give it a rest, are you?"

"No," Lee Ann said with unflinching honesty. "Yes and no, then."

"That's not good enough," Lee Ann said.

Katherine expelled a shaky breath. "I didn't think so."

"I'm waiting, and not very patiently, either."

"I ought to tell you to mind your own business," Katherine responded, glaring at her friend.

"Yeah, you could, but you won't. I think you need to talk. Right?"

Katherine tried to force herself to relax, but that was hard as she was so uptight. "I don't know what I need," she finally said in an unsteady tone.

"You need Bryce. He's been gone a week to that

ministerial conference, and that's what has you lower than a snake's belly.''

''You sure do know how to make a friend feel better.''

''Sure I do,'' Lee Ann said, smiling. Then it faded. ''Come on, quit stalling. It is Bryce, isn't it?''

''Okay, I miss him. Now are you satisfied?''

''Have you two got something going?''

''I guess you could say that.''

''Damn!''

''Lee Ann!''

''Sorry.''

She wasn't sorry at all, Katherine knew, but it didn't matter. That's what she was feeling, too, only she hadn't been able to express it. Her feelings were too jumbled to make any sense out of them at all.

When Bryce had told her he was leaving town for a week, she'd felt a sense of relief, stemming from the fact that she wouldn't have to see him for a while. Maybe then she could get her head back on straight, figure out how she really felt.

Instead, she had spent her time missing him, missing his calls, missing his spontaneous invitations, missing the hot, sensual look in his eye that he flashed her when no one else was looking, tossing them into a world all their own.

''Hey, I'm still here, in case you haven't noticed.''

Katherine gave a start. ''My mind went south.''

''Don't you mean north, where Bryce is?''

''All right, already,'' Katherine said tersely, getting up and walking to the fireplace. Once there, she turned and again, faced her friend who now had an odd look in her eyes.

"Are you in love with him?" Lee Ann asked in an almost-hushed tone.

Katherine shook her head. "I don't know."

"Hey, don't get me wrong, I think it would be great. I love him to death and you, too. But I would never have put the two of you together in a million years."

"Well, don't go joining us at the hip quite yet. We're really just friends."

Lee Ann rolled her eyes. "As in kissing friends, I'll bet."

Katherine's face became suffused with color, and she turned away.

"Ah, so I'm right. I'm also shocked as hell. I'll admit that."

Katherine swung around. "Believe it or not, I am, too, shocked that I would even give him the time of day."

"Oops," Lee Ann said suddenly, then stood. "I didn't realize it was so late. I have to be home and relieve Fred. But this conversation's far from over."

"Oh, yes it is, my friend. I've told you all there is to tell."

"For now, maybe."

"Permanently." Katherine paused. "You conned me into admitting that I miss him and haven't been seeing any other men because of him, but that doesn't mean he won't turn out to be a passing fancy like the others."

"Do you really believe that?"

"What I *know* is that I'm not cut out to even date a preacher, much less marry one. Also, he's beholden to all the people all the time, just like Jack."

"God, don't even mention those two in the same sentence."

"I know where you're going with that," Katherine replied, "and I agree. Still, Bryce is not the man for me."

Lee Ann blew out her breath as she loaded up the fabric books and walked to the door. "I guess we'll see what happens."

"I guess we will."

Lee Ann grinned. "You're a piece of work, you know, hiding him behind your back."

"Oh, get out of here."

Once Lee Ann and her laughter had disappeared, Katherine sank back onto the sofa, her legs having all the consistency of jelly. She couldn't believe she had confessed to seeing, then missing, Bryce. She stared at the phone wishing he'd call.

A deep sigh destroyed the silence as she let her head loll back onto the cushion. How had she ever gotten herself in this predicament? More to the point, how was she going to get out of it?

How was she going to get rid of the man who had become her heart's constant companion?

"Thanks for everything you did this week."

Bryce shook Dr. Milstead's hand. "Thank you for asking me, sir. The honor's all mine."

And it was. He'd been chosen by Milstead to be one of the main speakers throughout the week, which had elevated his position in the church's hierarchy. He'd been blessed all week and rejuvenated, as well. If Katherine had been with him, it would've been perfect. He grimaced at that thought.

"I'm counting on you to join us next year," Milstead was saying.

Bryce forced himself to pay attention. "The Lord willing, I'll be here."

"Good."

Milstead slapped Bryce on the back just before he got into his sport utility vehicle, slammed the door, waved, then drove off.

He was barely out of sight of the huge church in Dallas before his thoughts turned toward home and Katherine. Again he grimaced. Although she hadn't been off his mind the entire week, he hadn't called her.

He had decided not to see her anymore.

Suddenly Bryce gripped the steering wheel with all his strength. And because the decision had come from the head not the heart, he was hurting.

He was doing it for her as much as for himself. When the two older women had left his office, after more or less issuing an ultimatum that he stop seeing Katherine, he'd been as angry as he'd ever been in his life. He'd paced the floor until he'd almost worn another hole in the carpet.

Of course he had no intention of letting anyone dictate how he should run his personal life, he had told himself then and again now. He was responsible to God for his actions and no one else.

His conscience suddenly pricked him. That wasn't entirely true, and he knew it deep inside. He was responsible to the people in his church, the people who depended on him for their moral and spiritual guidance.

When he realized his hands were becoming numb on the steering wheel, he relaxed them. But nothing else relaxed. Every bone, every nerve in his body stayed tight.

He didn't know when he'd made his decision concerning Katherine. Maybe he'd known all along their relationship was an impossible one. Yet he'd plunged forward, anyway, because he'd been smitten with her. And still was.

But right now there were too many obstacles in the way, without mentioning Katherine herself, who had given him little reason to think she cared deeply for him. She did care, though, he was convinced of that. He had seen the way she'd looked at him. And she'd kissed him back, both times. That had not been his imagination.

She had been as hot for him as he had for her, which was not what solid relationships were built on. But what if he was in love with her? Could he leave her alone then?

If not, what was he willing to sacrifice for her?

He stared at the long road ahead before shoving his foot harder down on the accelerator.

Sixteen

Had he lost his mind? No. What he'd lost was his determination not to see her again.

It was nine o'clock, too late to be knocking on someone's door, most certainly Katherine's. He wiped a fine sheen of sweat from his upper lip as he rang the doorbell, hearing its lyrical sound from the outside.

What if she was asleep? He didn't think so, though, because the lamp was on in the living room. He could see its hazy glow. But some people left a light on all night, especially ones who lived alone.

Whatever the case, it was too late to turn chicken now. If she'd been asleep, she wasn't now. Not only was he sweating as if it was a hundred-degree summer day, but that knot in his gut was coiled so tightly he could feel it all the way to his throat.

Finally he heard her footsteps and knew he would soon be put out of his misery. She would let him in or tell him to hit the road. Either way, he'd have his answer.

The porch light flipped on, and she asked, "Who is it?"

He could hear the nervous edge in her voice, which was to be expected. "It's Bryce."

The dead bolt clicked, followed by the other lock, then the door swung open. Her eyes were wide, surprise mirrored in them. "Is something the matter?" she asked in a breathless tone.

"No."

"Then what—"

"May I come in?" he asked, interrupting her.

She toyed with her lower lip, a habit that drove him wild, as she moved to the side. "Of course."

Once they reached the middle of the room, they stopped and stared at each other. Now that he was with her, it hit home how much he'd really missed her. She was lovelier than ever, wearing a long silk robe.

Was she naked underneath?

His mouth turned dry as parchment at that thought. He could picture how lovely, how perfect her skin and curves would be.

"Bryce, are you all right?" she asked, that breathlessness still in her voice. "Has something happened?"

He swallowed hard. "No. Actually I just drove into town, so I don't know what's going on."

"You came here first."

He didn't know if she'd asked a question or made a statement. But it didn't matter. He was too busy drinking in her lovely face, a face that had haunted him since he'd left.

She kept staring as though she, too, was filling her eyes with him. "I'm glad you did," she said in a soft voice, lowering her head.

He cleared his throat, then gently tipped her chin to meet his heated gaze. "Are you? Are you really?"

"Yes."

He sucked in a shuddering breath as time seemed to stop. That was when he knew, in that moment, that he loved her and would love her to the day he died whether that be tomorrow or fifty years from now.

That truth slapped him upside the head with the force of a sledgehammer. The mental blow almost buckled his knees. Only the answering need in her eyes kept him upright. But what if he imagined it? What if he was so desperate to touch her, to hold her, that he was hallucinating?

"I had to come. I didn't mean to. I didn't want to but—" He paused, struggling for the right words, words that were clogged in his throat, choking him.

"But what?" she whispered.

"I couldn't stay away." She was bound to hear his heart. It was pounding so hard, he felt it in his ears. "I missed you," he said thickly.

"I…missed you, too."

Her unsteady admission, sounding as if it had been pulled from the depths of her, was his undoing. "Oh, Katherine," he rasped, reaching for her and folding her close in his arms.

For what seemed the longest time, their heartbeats merged as one. She felt so thin, so fragile in his arms, that he feared if he held her as tightly as he wanted, he'd crush her bones. He tried to smile, though it was lame at best. "Even when I slept, I missed you."

"Was I in your dreams?" Her voice sounded as though she was choking.

"All night."

"Do you remember them?"

"Every detail."

She circled her lips with the tip of her tongue, leaving them glistening with moisture. His response was instant and painful. The zipper took another pinch out of his burgeoning flesh.

"And in vivid color," he somehow managed to add.

A nail trailed down his chest, then back up. "Describe them."

What was happening to him? Whatever it was, it was like a sickness that had destroyed all coherent thought. He was working from pure sexual adrenaline. And it was exhilarating.

No doubt this woman standing before him had seized his mind, body and soul without even knowing it. And in record time, too.

"We were making love," he said at last.

"Always?"

"Always," he said, his senses spinning.

"Was I on top or bottom?"

He froze as though all the air had been knocked out of him. Fine madness. That was what this was all about. "Oh, Katherine," he whispered, seeking her lips that were wet and parted.

Their mouths clung, the kiss deepening with each passing second. Breaths mingled. Tongues tangled. Bodies molded.

Her breasts were crushed against his, allowing him the heady pleasure of feeling her nipples, now hard as small stones, pressing against the wall of his chest.

While continuing to hold her lips captive, he pushed a hand between them, slipping it inside her robe. When that hand connected with a bare breast, a strangled sound erupted.

She answered by clinging to him just before she gently disengaged herself and untied the sash on her robe, giving him free access to her body.

He tried to speak, but he couldn't. The exquisite beauty of her body deprived him of the breath to speak. All he could do was stare.

"Katherine."

He didn't realize he'd spoken until she whispered, "No one's ever said my name quite like you."

"You're lovely."

Her response was to reach up and place her lips against his. Later he realized it was her taking control that shot his emotions out of control.

He adhered her to him, running his hands down her back, over her buttocks, squeezing the cheeks until she was as close as she could be without him being inside her.

She groaned, then pulled back as if to get her breath from that long, sucking kiss, only to reach for the belt on his pants.

In a frenzy to feel flesh against flesh he stilled her fingers and said in a guttural voice, "Let me."

Within seconds his clothes were discarded, and he had his wish—skin against skin, lips against lips. Unable to make it to the bedroom, he pulled her with him to the carpet. Once there, close to the simmering fireplace, he leaned over and nibbled at her neck, inhaling the scent of her flesh, feeling himself grow dizzier with each touch.

"If I ever got my hands on you, I told myself, I'd kiss you all over."

"Oh, Bryce," she whispered.

"And lick your breasts, lick you all over."

"Oh, yes, yes." Her whisper turned into a muted cry.

The tip of his tongue circled one breast, the other. When she began to squirm, he licked, then sucked a nipple, feeling it expand against his lips.

"Oh, please!"

Her needy cry added more fuel to the raging fire already burning inside him. "Please what?"

"Stop torturing me," she said in a pleading voice, her eyes glazed with desire.

"Oh, honey, I'm just getting started."

Having said that, he slid his tongue down her flat belly, dipping in and out of her naval before moving to the crisp curls between her thighs. As if of their own volition, her thighs parted, giving his lips and tongue access to the sweetness there.

When his tongue nudged the tender bud, she lurched, grabbed a handful of his hair and cried out.

Once he knew she had climaxed, he lifted himself over her and, holding her gaze, entered her, hard, fast and high. Arching her back, she met him thrust for thrust until they both moaned simultaneously and he collapsed on top of her.

Katherine felt him stir beside her, only to then realize they were in her bed. Because she wasn't on her usual side, she couldn't see the clock. Bryce's body was in the way.

Careful not to rouse him just yet, she lifted her head just enough to see the lit digital numbers. Five o'clock.

She eased her head back down and for a moment lay still and listened to his breathing. The moon shone through the sheers, granting her the privilege of seeing his face. She simply stared at him for the longest time, every nerve inside her body alive, as if she had just been hit by a bolt of electricity.

She had. Him.

Holding back a shuddering breath, she concentrated on his long, thick eyelashes, the kind she or any woman would kill to have. Her gaze moved to the curve of his strong jaw, which bore signs of a five-o'clock shadow, down to his chest, matted with dark hair—hair that she had run her fingers through countless times before their marathon lovemaking had ended.

Did he know how to love a woman or what?

When he'd been inside her, filling her completely, all rational thought had fled her mind. Nothing mattered except him and the incredible things he was doing to her body.

Love?

Was that what this was all about? She prayed not— for him and for her. Sex. She had to believe that was all it was for both of them, considering the circumstances. And there was nothing wrong with that. They were two adults who could do pretty much as they pleased.

Wrong.

Her stomach lurched. He was a preacher, and she was a divorced woman. Like oil and water they didn't mix, would never mix.

Don't, she told herself. Don't go there, to that secret place in her heart where all her torrid emotions were stored under lock and key.

For the moment she wanted them to stay there. Later she could open that door, in the daylight, when she was alone, and examine all those painful issues.

Now she only wanted to experience more of that sexual rush that only he could give her and she could give him. Facing him, she outlined his lips with the tip of her tongue.

He started, then his eyes popped open. A sensual expression jumped into them.

"Katherine—"

"Don't talk. Just enjoy."

With that she slowly nibbled and bit her way down his hard body, beginning at his chest. Only when she reached his swollen manhood and surrounded it did he groan out loud and clutch at her.

"Oh, my Katherine," he chanted as though in blissful agony before pulling her up then down onto him. With his eyes on her face and his hands on her breasts, she began moving at a frantic pace. Moments later, feeling him spill his seed into her, she collapsed on top of him.

After he'd eased her off him onto her side and they were facing each other, legs still entwined, Bryce said, "I'm happier right now than I've been in a long time, maybe ever."

"Good sex will do that to you every time," she said lightly, more lightly than she felt.

His features darkened. "It's more than sex, at least it is for me."

"Me, too," she admitted in a faltering voice.

"Did he make you happy at all?" Bryce asked without warning.

She stiffened, not at all eager to talk about Jack, not because she still cared, either. He just wasn't worth the effort or the energy. "At first, but he never—" She stopped.

"He never what?" Bryce urged, sounding almost desperate.

"He never gave himself like you, let himself go." She paused. "There was a part of him he always held back."

"Were you sorry about that, I mean?"

"No. Jack was not a nice man."

"He hurt you, didn't he? Physically, I'm talking about."

Katherine wasn't surprised that he finally hit her with the truth that he'd guessed early on. After all, he was a minister who was in tune with people and intuitive to boot.

"Yes, he did," she admitted. "It was after he found out that he couldn't father a child that our marriage went from bad to worse."

She paused again, and he pulled her closer. "He took his anger and humiliation out on me, becoming even more possessive and obsessive, positive that I was going to leave him for someone else."

"That's not you."

"You're right, but he never saw that. Anyway, one morning he went into a rage and struck me."

Bryce sucked in a harsh breath, but he didn't interrupt.

"I told him if he ever did that again, I'd kill him. Then I packed my bags and walked out. That was six years ago."

"Have you been serious about anyone since?"

"No. How about you?"

"I've taken several women out, but that's all. Until now, that is."

The room fell suddenly silent as did her heart.

"Bryce—"

"I love you, Katherine. I fell in love with you the

first time I saw you, only I didn't realize it until I walked into your house last night.''

"Bryce, I don't know what to say."

"What's in your heart," he said in a low, thick tone. When she didn't respond right off, he went on, "I want you to marry me."

"Oh, Bryce, I still don't know what to say."

"It's simple. Just say yes."

Seventeen

"Katherine, I asked you a question, a very important one." Bryce paused. "Or at least I thought so."

She picked up on the disguised pain in his voice and hated that she was the cause of it.

Once he'd popped the question to her, she had given him a quick look, then without answering had disentangled herself, reached for her robe that lay at the foot of the bed, slipped into it and gotten up.

Holding the silence, Bryce had followed suit, striding into the living room where his clothes remained heaped on the floor. Once he had slipped into his underwear, shirt and slacks, he'd joined her in the kitchen where she was busy making coffee, anything that would occupy her mind and steady her hands.

Now, though, she couldn't put off answering him any longer. Underneath that pain, she'd also noted a hint of steel.

"We have to talk," she said.

"I thought that was what we were doing in bed."

She flushed for no reason at all, which brought a fleeting smile to his face before it disappeared.

Her breathing turned shallow, and her heart was beating far faster than normal. "You know what I mean," she said in a low tone.

"So again, will you marry me?"

They were facing each other across her breakfast room table, mugs filled with steaming coffee in front of them. But neither was drinking. They were too busy drinking in each other.

"Have you thought this through, Bryce?"

"Will you stop answering me with a question?"

"I'm sorry."

"No, you're not." He smiled again, but as before it didn't last long.

She lowered her eyes to the coffee cup.

"Katherine."

His sexy voice followed by a hand covering hers sent another shaft of longing through her. She lifted her eyes and met his, which were spilling over with that same longing.

But she wouldn't give way to that feeling at the moment. Besides, she sensed sex was not uppermost in his mind, either. Right now he was like a blood-hound with a one-track mind.

"I can't answer you, that's the problem."

He withdrew his hand and expelled a sigh. "I see."

"No, you don't."

"All right, I don't." He paused and delved back into her eyes. "Do you love me?"

"Yes," she admitted with a full heart.

"Then I don't see the problem."

"I need more time."

"Why?" he asked, his tone low and not quite steady.

"It's happened all too quickly for me." She paused and leaned her head to one side. "And for you, too. You can't deny that."

"You're right, I can't."

She shook her head. "Bryce, I'm divorced. I can't imagine what your mother and others—"

"Stop," he said, covering her hand again. "Don't worry about my mother or anyone else for that matter. I'm well aware that you're divorced, and while I would've preferred otherwise, that's the way it is."

"But others might not accept it."

"Then that's their problem."

"Oh, Bryce, it's just not that simple."

"So what are you saying?"

"That I need more time," she said. "The thought of marrying a minister boggles my mind. I'm a sinful party girl, for heaven's sake."

A grin suddenly brightened his heretofore dull features. "You don't have the market cornered on sin, my darling. Whether you're divorced or a party girl isn't the issue. Love is the issue here. And now that we've made love, I can't let you go.''

"Are you sorry about that?'' Her voice faltered again.

"Absolutely not. But for me, love and commitment go hand in hand. When I made love to you,'' he added in a husky tone, "I made a lifetime commitment to you.''

"Oh, Bryce.'' She fought back the tears that stung the back of her eyes.

"Hey, what are those tears all about?''

"For you life is so uncomplicated, so black-and-white. It's not that way for me. There are a lot of gray areas.''

"And our relationship falls into the gray area. Is that what you're saying?'' His gaze was probing.

"At this moment it does.''

He released a harsh sigh. "What if you're pregnant?''

"I'm not.''

"Are you on the Pill?''

"No.''

"Then how do you know?''

"A woman just knows. It's not the right time of the month.''

Their eyes met for another long second, then he stood. "I'll give you the time you want, but just don't take too long.'' An uneven breath escaped him before he leaned over and gave her a deep kiss. "I love you. Just keep that in mind while you're playing in that gray area.''

With that he walked out, leaving her sitting, a tight band around her heart, threatening to squeeze the life out of it.

Two weeks later that tight band was still there. In fact, Katherine feared she might have permanent damage if something didn't give.

She loved him, no doubt about it, but did she love him enough to marry him, to change her way of life? That question had haunted her day and night since he'd walked out of her house.

True to his word, he hadn't pushed her, though she'd seen the pain and impatience in his eyes when they had been together, which was often.

Business was booming at the shop. It was October, and customers were already well into their Christmas shopping. Too, things were popping at the church, meaning she spent a lot of her evenings there with Lee Ann, and finally all the choices of fabric, wall coverings, flooring and furniture were chosen.

Following those sessions she would see Bryce alone. Although he would kiss her with deep passion and longing, he hadn't made love to her. As a result, tension had increased and nerves were raw.

Katherine realized she couldn't remain in this limbo of indecision for much longer.

"Hey, how's it going, kid?"

It was after closing time, but she hadn't locked the shop as yet, so Lee Ann just breezed in.

Katherine gave her friend a lame smile. "I'm pooped. What about you?"

"Same here. I was on my way to the grocery store and saw that you were still here."

"Not for long."

"Are you seeing Bryce tonight?"

"Do you have a second?"

"Sure. Fred's making dinner tonight."

After they reached the back, Katherine poured their coffee. "Something's up. What is it?"

"Bryce asked me to marry him."

Lee Ann's jaw dropped. "You're not serious."

"Would I joke about a thing like that?"

"No," Lee Ann said, "you wouldn't. I knew things were heating up, but marriage—"

"It's mind-boggling, isn't it?"

"If I remember correctly, I asked you if you loved him, and you said you didn't know. Has that changed?"

Katherine didn't hesitate. "Yes. I finally admitted to myself I love him, but as we both know, love does not conquer all, not in the real world, that is."

"He's a wonderful man."

"I know that, too," Katherine said with an unwanted shiver. "But I'm afraid I'll fail him and in turn cause him to fail."

"Well, as your friend, I feel I have to tell you this."

"What?"

"Hey, take it easy. It's not earth-shattering."

"What?" Katherine demanded again, not bothering to temper her impatience.

"A couple of old biddies in the church have been giving Bryce flak about you."

Katherine felt as if she'd been kicked in the stomach, yet she wasn't surprised. "I tried to tell him that something like that might happen, but he wouldn't listen."

"He loves you, my friend. That's so obvious every time he looks at you."

"I'd like to wring their necks for making things tough for him. But at the same time, it reinforces my fears about marrying a person who's always under someone else's watchful eye."

"I hear you."

"Too, I don't want to do anything that will jeopardize his career and his commitment to his work."

"Look, I wish I had an answer, but I don't. All I can do is be here for you and listen."

Katherine gave her a lackluster smile. "I appreciate that more than you'll know. Now, you'd best skedaddle and get on home."

Lee Ann stood, then kissed her on the cheek. "Praying about this matter certainly wouldn't hurt."

Katherine smiled through uninvited tears and said softly, "That's the best idea yet."

When he walked in the door of her house the following evening, Katherine caught her breath. As always, in a confined space, she was aware of his tall, muscled body. And though he looked good, she knew he tasted much better.

Sudden heat rose into her cheeks, and it wasn't from the warmth of the fireplace, either.

"You're up to something," Bryce said, tossing his coat down and coming toward her, a glint in his eyes.

"What makes you say that?" she asked in a breathless voice, his cologne activating her senses even more.

"It's simple. Your cheeks turn rosy."

"You could be wrong, you know."

"But I'm not," he said thickly, that glint deepening as he bore down on her.

"You're just too cocky for your own good."

"Come here," he muttered, grabbing her, then opening his moist, hard lips against hers. She reveled in the sweet pressure of those lips and his hard body that seemed to align with hers as if he'd just found the missing piece to the puzzle.

When he finally pulled back and pushed her to arm's length, he was pale and his breathing labored. "I was about to have dessert before the meal."

"Would that be so bad?" Her tone was teasing, but her eyes were not. She longed for him to make love to her again and was upset that he hadn't.

"I want you, too," he said, voicing her hidden thoughts, "more than you can imagine."

He took her hand and placed it over the zipper of his jeans. He was full and hard. He groaned when she began to move her palm up and down.

"Oh, Katherine—"

"Oh, Katherine, what?" she whispered, not taking

her eyes off his face, watching the myriad expressions on it.

When two fingers settled on the zipper, he stilled them, and stared at her through glazed eyes. "Say you'll marry me," he ground out.

She removed her hand and stepped back. "You promised you wouldn't push."

He shoved a hand through his hair and smiled, but it was forced, she knew. The veins in his neck were standing out and a muscle was ticking overtime in his jaw. He had a tight rein on his control. She wondered what he'd do if she pushed him to the sexual limit.

"Sorry. I'll back off."

She was barely able to hide her disappointment. "Are you ready to eat?"

"Lead the way."

A short time later, after the kitchen was straight, they were back in the living room, on the sofa, in front of the fire, facing each other, but not touching.

Although he told her everything was good, she doubted he'd enjoyed a bite he ate. She knew *she* hadn't. Everything had tasted like cardboard.

Now, as they looked at each other, she realized that she had to give him an answer, that she'd toyed with his and her emotions long enough. Still—

"Katherine—"

"Why didn't you tell me there was gossip about us?" She didn't mean to blurt that out. It just came unbidden from her lips.

He straightened his legs, got to his feet and walked

to the fireplace. When he turned back around, his face was without emotion. "I didn't see the need."

"Why not?"

"Because it's my problem."

Her lips tightened. "How can you say that when it affects me, too?"

"I'm the one who has to deal with it."

"That's the point." Her voice cracked. "You shouldn't have to deal with it."

He strode back to the sofa, sat down and took both her hands in his. "Listen to me. I'll willingly go find another church, rather than give you up."

"Oh, Bryce," she cried softly, "I would never let you do that."

"But I love you, and making sacrifices is part of love."

"Not that kind of sacrifice, giving up your church, especially after you've worked so hard to get a new sanctuary."

"There's another sanctuary waiting to be built somewhere else."

This time she got up and walked to the fireplace, her heart burdened beyond belief.

"A few members' disapproval has changed nothing, Katherine. If anything, I want to marry you more now than ever."

"I can't, Bryce, or at least not right now."

He flinched visibly, and the color receded from his face.

She turned away, unable to look at him, but plunged on before her courage and her good sense completely deserted her. "What's more, I'll never be able to marry again."

He stood, his jaws clamped together, hurt and pain radiating from his eyes. "Well, you can rest assured I won't try and force you into doing something that you don't want to do."

"So, do I have another reprieve?"

"No."

Her stomach clenched. "No?"

"I think it's best I leave you alone. It sounds like that's what you want." He made his way to the door where he paused, his eyes bleak. "I hope you find what you're looking for, Katherine. Obviously it's not me."

Long after he'd gone and the fire burned out, sobs racked her body.

Eighteen

Katherine thought she knew how it felt to be truly miserable, to be totally disillusioned with life, when she'd gone through the trauma with Jack. But she had been wrong. What she was going through now was far worse.

Once again her life had been turned upside down. When Bryce had walked out, promising not to bother her anymore, something had broken inside her.

And it was still broken despite the fact that it had been two months since she'd seen him, the longest two months of her life.

Oh, she had functioned like a normal human, or at least she felt as though she had, though at times Nancy had sure given her some strange glances.

"Is everything okay?" Nancy had even asked just the other day.

"Everything's fine," Katherine lied. "I guess I'm just tired."

"No wonder, at the pace you've been keeping lately, with getting ready to open the new store and all."

"It's been a major undertaking, I'll admit."

Nancy's face clouded. "I'm sorry I'm not more available, but—"

"Hey, you don't have to keep apologizing. You've got your family back together and you need to spend more time with them. I'm delighted for you."

And she was. Thanks to Bryce and his gentle and steady counseling of both Nancy and her husband, a family had been glued back together, hopefully forever.

If only...

Stop that, she told herself. She had made her choice to remain single, to make her career the main focus of her life. With that in mind, she had poured her heart and soul into finding a location for a second store, secured the loan at the bank and found a neat lady to run it.

The church renovations were well underway, and the offices and parlor were going to be stunning. Although the hands-on work had ended, there were still things that came up that she or Lee Ann had to see about. If that lot fell to her, she made sure she didn't run into Bryce.

Surprisingly, she'd had her share of pats on the

back for her work there. Several of the church women, maybe even the ones who had been so critical of her and Bryce's relationship, had held a coffee partly in her and Lee Ann's honor.

Katherine had been quite touched, especially when one had come up to her and said, ''My dear, we all hope that you'll become a permanent part of our church. We would love to have you.''

Katherine knew that invitation had come from the lady's heart. Due to the circumstances, there was no way she could join that church even if she wanted to.

In addition to work as a panacea for her broken life, she had become addicted to physical fitness. In the evenings she would either go to the gym and work out or stay at home and run three miles in the neighborhood.

She couldn't deny that her life was full, that she didn't have a wasted moment in any of her days. Then, why was she so damn miserable? Why was her full life not worth living?

Bryce.

She missed him terribly. When she thought about him, the pain that pierced her heart was so sharp she stopped dead in her tracks. So what was she going to do?

Nothing.

For both their sakes she had done the right thing. She had to believe that or she couldn't go on.

Suddenly she jerked herself out of her morbid thoughts and back to the moment at hand. Shortly she was to meet and have dinner with a lingerie salesman who had convinced her to try his new line, a line that she was very excited about.

The dinner part she could've done without, but he'd insisted. And because he was a friend who was happily married with three children, she had decided to go.

What harm could possibly come of that?

"The food was delicious, Frank."

Frank Calhoun grinned, his big mouth opening to a row of equally big white teeth. Despite the fact that his ruddy skin and large features didn't make him an attractive package, he was nonetheless one of the nicest men she'd dealt with.

"I thought so myself. For a town this size, this restaurant's damn good."

"It's practically the only decent place to eat, if you want some ambiance, that is."

"Well, again, you chose well."

"Thanks. It was good for me to get out."

He gave her a strange look at the same time quirking one bushy eyebrow quirked. "You act like you've become a nun."

She smiled with no warmth.

"What's happened to that feisty redhead who used to kick up her heels on a nightly basis?"

"That's an exaggeration," she countered with forced lightness.

"Not much of one. So answer my question."

"I'd rather not," she said bluntly.

His eyes narrowed, then he grinned. "It's a man.

That's the only thing that can give a woman that 'look.'"

"Hey, you're treading on soft ground."

Frank's grin widened. "Won't be the first time." He sobered. "In all seriousness, I hate to see you unhappy."

"Who says I'm unhappy?"

"It shows, Katherine," he said in a low, brusque tone.

That was almost her undoing. Unexpected tears welled up the back of her throat. "Frank, I—"

"Enough said, at least from me. I'll shut my mouth. But whoever's responsible is a damn fool."

She smiled, only to have that smile suddenly freeze on her face as she saw a couple standing at the front, waiting to be seated by the hostess.

Oh, God, no, it couldn't be, she told herself. But it was. Bryce in the flesh. With another woman. Quickly Katherine averted her gaze, wishing she could disappear.

"Katherine, what the hell?" Frank demanded. "You look as if someone just cut your throat."

"Someone just did," she muttered, then realizing what she'd said, added in a shaky voice, "Don't mind me."

He gave her a keen look. "Do you wanna go?"

"Please, if you don't mind."

She stood, and that was when he saw her. She wanted to turn away again, not meet his gaze, but she couldn't. Even though she'd been dealt a brutal blow, she was drawn to him like a magnet. She didn't know how long their eyes held before he nodded, then smiled coolly.

It was that cool smile that jarred her into motion. "I'm ready," she said tersely, then walked out, her head held high.

Later, in her bed, Katherine lay curled into a fetal position, crushed in body and spirit. Yet, she was mad, too. Damn him, she cried silently, only then to think how awful it was to damn a minister.

Yet he was a man. And it was that part of him that had hurt her deeply. How could he see another woman? How could he touch someone else the way he'd touched her? That thought took another chunk out of her heart.

The woman aside, seeing him was traumatic in itself. It brought back all the longing and desire she had suppressed. And her love for him—it was stronger than ever.

But what about him? Did he still love her? Or had he written her off as a hopeless case and found someone else, like that woman he'd been with, someone who was more suitable for a minister's wife?

Realizing that she had blown it, that she'd given up the best thing that could've ever happened to her, Katherine squeezed the pillow and buried her head in it, letting the pent-up tears have free rein.

"You have a staff meeting in fifteen minutes."
Bryce turned and faced his secretary, who stood in

the door of his makeshift office. ''Thanks. Believe it or not, I hadn't forgotten.''

''Maybe it won't be much longer until you're out of this cubbyhole.''

''That's on my prayer list for sure.''

She laughed, then stepped out and closed the door.

Bryce's features turned serious once again as he faced the window. It was raining, a cold, steady rain that had started during the middle of the night. He knew because he was awake.

A sigh came from deep within him. Since he'd lost Katherine, he hadn't slept one night through. His modus operandi was to toss and turn and catch a few cat naps in between.

When he got up each morning, his bed looked like a war zone. Another sigh escaped him. He would give anything if he hadn't encountered her at the restaurant, but he had. The wound inside him had in no way closed; it was still raw and extremely painful.

Seeing her looking lovelier than he'd even remembered had caused that wound to start oozing again. Thank God the man she'd been with was a salesman; the inscribed briefcases sitting beside him had labeled him as such.

Still, it had rankled, her being with any man, a business associate or not. He wondered what she had thought when she had seen him with a woman. Had it bothered her? He would like to think it had, even though his dinner engagement was as innocent as hers.

His first cousin, Natalie, who had been like a sister

to him when he was growing up, had come to town. His mother, who hadn't been feeling well, had insisted they have dinner together and catch up on old times.

But once he'd seen Katherine, the joy had gone out of the evening.

Dear Lord, he loved her, and couldn't imagine how he was going to live the rest of his life without her. But what could he do? He couldn't force her to change her mind. He couldn't force her to love him in spite of his vocation.

Suddenly Bryce doubled his fists, feeling as though he could hit something and feel better. He knew that wasn't the case. Only time would heal his pain and loss. After all, he had recovered from Molly's death.

He could do so again. Or could he? Somehow he didn't think so. He would love Katherine and only her until the day he died.

"You're the stubbornest, most hardheaded woman I know."

Katherine scowled at the phone. "I didn't call to ask you over for lunch to get chewed out, Lee Ann."

"I could apologize."

"Only you're not." A semblance of a smile softened Katherine's lips.

"Right."

A silence ensued on the phone line as Katherine repositioned herself on the sofa.

"He's miserable, you know," Lee Ann said at last.

Katherine's stomach suddenly rebelled. She thought

she might lose the light dinner she'd just eaten. "Don't start again, please."

"I just hate to see two people I love so miserable."

"How can you say that when he was with another woman, for God's sake?" Katherine said.

"At least you're jealous. That's a good sign."

"This conversation's going nowhere fast."

"I don't profess to know who he was with or why, but I can tell you this, she's not his lover."

"How do you know?"

"He doesn't work that way."

Katherine was quiet for another moment.

"So forget the 'other woman' thing. Since you broke it off with him, he's hurting, Katherine, really badly, though he tries to cover it."

"I'm hurting, too."

"Then do something about it."

Hours later, long after she had talked to her friend, Katherine remained in the same position, her friend's parting words ringing in her ears. She didn't want to live without Bryce. She realized that now. But what could she do about it?

Go to him.

That thought almost stopped her breathing. If she listened to the voice in her soul, what could she say to him? The truth. She would tell him that she loved him, that she had let what one man did to her cloud her vision and her heart to the goodness and kindness in another.

It also hit her full force that her shop, her leisure activities, her freedom made for a very empty future compared to her love for Bryce. How could she give up relying on his strength as well as having his big warm body next to hers through the good as well as the bad?

She couldn't. It was just that simple.

But a minister?

The very idea of being married to one sent another ripple of doubt through her. But that doubt disappeared when she got slapped up side the head with another two-by-four. It was Bryce's vocation that made him the trustworthy and irresistible man he was, the man she loved.

With the love of a man like that behind her, she could overcome anything.

Suddenly Katherine lunged off the sofa, grabbed her purse and darted out of the house. She just prayed she wasn't too late.

"Bryce."

She knocked again. More silence. She knew that he was home, since she was staring at his car, which was parked in the drive in front of hers.

Maybe he knew it was her and wasn't going to answer the door. No. That wasn't Bryce's way, either. No matter what she had done to him, he had more integrity than that.

The door opened and he was there, and suddenly she didn't know what to say. She stood in front of him and stared, her tongue stuck to the roof of her mouth.

"Do you want to come in?" he asked, his voice sounding lower and thicker than usual, like rich syrup.

She swallowed her panic, nodded, then stepped across the threshold. Though his gaze seemed to hold no animosity, his body was stiff as if he were holding himself in check.

It appeared as if she was going to have to work for forgiveness, which was all right, if that was what it took to get him back.

"Am I too late, Bryce?" she whispered, peering up at him from her soul.

He took a step toward her, only to pull up short. "For what?"

"To tell you that I love you."

He grabbed her then and buried her face against his trembling body. "Oh, Katherine, it's never too late for those words."

She pulled back, her face drenched with tears. "I saw you with that woman and thought I'd lost you forever."

"That woman was my first cousin."

"Oh."

He laughed outright, then kissed her with deep-felt passion and tenderness. "You're going to make one helluva preacher's wife."

"Bryce!" she exclaimed, her eyes wide with shock at his choice of words.

He laughed again. "Let's get married."

"When?"

"First thing in the morning."

"What about tonight?" she asked in a breathless tone.

His eyes darkened. "You're not going anywhere, young lady. I'm not ever letting you out of my sight again."

Six Months Later

"Oh, Bryce, I can't believe I'm so happy."

He chuckled, then tapped her on the nose.

"You're one of a kind, my darling. Only you would be so bluntly truthful."

They were facing each other on the king-size bed that might as well have been a twin as they were never more than a breath away from the other.

"That's why you love me, isn't it?"

His voice dropped several degrees, along with his eyes. "That and a whole lot more. The fact that you trusted me enough to fly with me is just one of the 'mores.'"

Katherine made a face at him. "Well, I'll admit I had butterflies the size of our state in my stomach, but it wasn't too bad." She gave him a sassy grin.

His eyes darkened. "Ah, while we're on the subject of stomachs, butterflies are not the only thing that's in yours."

"So you're not unhappy about the baby?"

"If I had my way, I'd keep you barefoot and pregnant all the time." He paused. "What about you?"

"I'm scared but thrilled."

He leaned over suddenly and kissed her still-flat stomach before moving up to suckle a breast.

"Oh, Bryce," she murmured, nestling her hands in his hair while her body quivered under his warm, questing lips.

"I want you again," he rasped, seeking her eyes.

Wordlessly she eased her legs apart and he eased inside her, and with them still facing each other, he thrust deeply and kept on thrusting until their cries colored the air.

Later, he pulled back but not out of her. "I don't think I'll ever get enough of you."

"Neither will I."

And she wouldn't. She was convinced of that. In fact, she could rewrite the definition of *happiness* since she'd been married to Bryce. Many of the fears she had harbored about being a pastor's wife had disappeared the moment he had introduced her to his members as his wife.

They had embraced her with open arms, especially his mother whom she'd come to love and who returned her love without reservation.

Of course, Lee Ann and Nancy had been delighted, especially Lee Ann, who took credit for bringing them together as man and wife.

If there was a barb in their life, it was her work. Often she felt guilty for spending more time at her shops than she did at the church.

It was that guilt nudging her that made her ask, "Would you really have resigned your job rather than give me up?"

Bryce gave her a shocked look. "I can't believe you're asking me that now."

"Well, I am."

He smiled, then shook his head. "Yes, my darling. I meant ever word."

"So should I do the same?"

He pulled back a bit. "What on earth are you talking about?"

"My shops. Should I give them up and become a full-time pastor's wife and mother?"

A silence suddenly filled the room, during which she heard his uneven breathing. "Do you want to?"

"No."

"I don't want you to, either," he said with sincerity.

"Then why do I feel so guilty?"

"I don't know, but you shouldn't."

"Well, I am going to cut way back, now that I'm pregnant." Her voice suddenly held a tremor. "I can't believe I'm going to have a baby. Me, the one who said no husband, no children, no house with a white picket fence around it."

He laughed. "And what do you have?"

"All three," she cried, "and I'm loving it."

"Praise the Lord!"

They both laughed as they turned to each other in love.

*   *   *   *   *

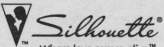

You're not going to believe this offer!

In October and November 2000, buy any two Harlequin or Silhouette books and save $10.00 off future purchases, or buy any three and save $20.00 off future purchases!

Just fill out this form and attach 2 proofs of purchase (cash register receipts) from October and November 2000 books and Harlequin will send you a coupon booklet worth a total savings of $10.00 off future purchases of Harlequin and Silhouette books in 2001. Send us 3 proofs of purchase and we will send you a coupon booklet worth a total savings of $20.00 off future purchases.

Saving money has never been this easy.

I accept your offer! Please send me a coupon booklet:

Name: _____

Address: _____ City: _____

State/Prov.: _____ Zip/Postal Code: _____

Optional Survey!

In a typical month, how many Harlequin or Silhouette books would you buy <u>new</u> at retail stores?

☐ Less than 1   ☐ 1   ☐ 2   ☐ 3 to 4   ☐ 5+

Which of the following statements best describes how you <u>buy</u> Harlequin or Silhouette books? Choose one answer only that <u>best</u> describes you.

☐ I am a regular buyer and reader
☐ I am a regular reader but buy only occasionally
☐ I only buy and read for specific times of the year, e.g. vacations
☐ I subscribe through Reader Service but also buy at retail stores
☐ I mainly borrow and buy only occasionally
☐ I am an occasional buyer and reader

Which of the following statements best describes how you <u>choose</u> the Harlequin and Silhouette series books you buy <u>new</u> at retail stores? By "series," we mean books within a particular line, such as *Harlequin PRESENTS* or *Silhouette SPECIAL EDITION*. Choose one answer only that <u>best</u> describes you.

☐ I only buy books from my favorite series
☐ I generally buy books from my favorite series but also buy books from other series on occasion
☐ I buy some books from my favorite series but also buy from many other series regularly
☐ I buy all types of books depending on my mood and what I find interesting and have no favorite series

Please send this form, along with your cash register receipts as proofs of purchase, to:
In the U.S.: Harlequin Books, P.O. Box 9057, Buffalo, NY 14269
In Canada: Harlequin Books, P.O. Box 622, Fort Erie, Ontario L2A 5X3
(Allow 4-6 weeks for delivery) Offer expires December 31, 2000.   PHQ4002

Silhouette® —

where love comes alive—online...

eHARLEQUIN.com

your romantic life

—Romance 101—
♥ Guides to romance, dating and flirting.

—Dr. Romance—
♥ Get romance advice and tips from
our expert, Dr. Romance.

—Recipes for Romance—
♥ How to plan romantic meals for you
and your sweetie.

—Daily Love Dose—
♥ Tips on how to keep the romance
alive every day.

—Tales from the Heart—
♥ Discuss romantic dilemmas with other
members in our Tales from the Heart
message board.